Rebel Wife

Perle Butcher Lyon

Inknbeans Press

Cover art: Evonne, the art elf

ISBN-13: 978-0692581131 (Inknbeans Press)

ISBN-10: 0692581138

Contents

Chapter One 1

Chapter Two 26

Chapter Three 52

Chapter Four 81

Chapter Five 106

Chapter Six 130

Chapter Seven 154

Chapter Eight 181

Chapter Nine 207

Chapter Ten 229

About the Author 255

More From Inknbeans Press 256

Chapter One
The Chaos

The dust swirled up on the dirt road as the people rushed along, stinging eyes and making muddy trails in the heavily perspiring faces. "Is it true?" I demanded urgently of each person in the crush who looked as if he or she might speak English. "Please," I cried, tugging one man's tattered sleeve. "Are they coming? Has the revolution come here?"

He turned slightly, gave me a wide-eyed stare and pulled his arm free with such ferocity that a bit of the fabric of his shirt stuck to my fingers. Buffeted by the crowd, I turned around, looking for someone else to ask. Another man, clearly not a native, was pushing his way through the crowd, a valise clutched under one arm, his free hand on his head, holding a white Panama hat in place. "Sir, is it-"

"I have no time. I have a train to catch." He shouldered his way past me. "Out of my way."

I staggered backwards, falling against a brick wall of a man. "Oh!" I gasped as a strong brown came around my waist. Twisting around, I recognized my keeper as the captain of the military junta that had overtaken the small Central American country the year before. I had seen him many times – a black haired, black eyed dragon, striding through the streets of what passed for a town, a riding crop snapping against his leg in a loud and frightening crack. The green billed hat with its gleaming medals a crown to lord his position over the poor, hungry, and hungry that inhabited his domain now dipped low, over his eyes, as the sun rose over the tin roof of the railroad station. "Perhaps you can tell me, Captain Contreras," I asked coldly, putting my hands on his arm to push him away, "has there finally been uprising?"

He released me with a jerk, those black eyes flicking back to the hysterical exodus before him. "A small insurrection, *Senorita*," he answered arrogantly. "It will be controlled within a few days. It is nothing for your concern."

"If there is nothing to be worried about, why are we all being chased out of the country like the neighbor's bad little boy?" I demanded, trying to smooth wrinkles and dust from my khaki shirt.

He frowned, puzzled, as if he was momentarily distracted from the flow of humanity, by some upstart girl glaring up at him. "I do not understand your question, *Senorita*," he admitted, this time letting his eyes slide down my body, making me cringe inwardly.

"Why are we being forced to leave?" I repeated impatiently as I swatted at one of the blue winged flies that hovered constantly in the air around us.

He sighed, equally impatient and seemingly impervious to the flies, which were known to have a nasty bite. "It is a military emergency, not a holiday. We cannot have tourists strolling around in the middle of gunfire. Accidents could happen." He shrugged.

"So, the conflict is coming," I concluded.

His jaw clenched for a moment, and it made a vein stand out under the dark skin of his neck. "Your government has asked us to return all of its citizens."

So it was true. I'd been hearing rumors that the U.S. was sending in soldiers in an effort to cease hostilities between the military government and the rebellion which had been attempting to overthrow it for two years. "Then, perhaps you could-"

"I don't have time for this," he interrupted, gesturing with the riding crop. "Get your things together, *Senorita*," he commanded. "The train is coming."

I was tempted to ignore him, but if the U.S. was withdrawing all its citizens, how would that affect the members of the Peace Corps here? "Very well, Captain Contreras," I agreed, moving away from him with a mutinous glare. As a nurse, I was loathe to leave the tiny village. In the few months I had been here, I had already seen the gross abuse inflicted by the military dictatorship which felt guns and drug money gave them the right to murder, rape and terrorize. However, I had also learned to avoid crossing paths with any of the soldiers if it could possibly be helped. Chivalry had died in infancy here. Women had only one purpose for these men.

"*Senorita*, wait," the captain ordered, taking a step toward me.

I turned, poised for flight. "Yes, Captain?" I suppose I made a mockery of the title, in spite of myself.

He was frowning at me, but it didn't appear to be enraged. "You know my name," he said. "How is that?"

"Oh, really, Captain," I laughed sardonically. I was not naturally brave or defiant, but I was very tired and a little frightened, and known not to be entirely rational under those conditions. "Doesn't everyone in this little jungle know the great *Capitan* Contreras? Doesn't the mere breath of his name make us quiver with fear?" The idea that I was being forced onto a train and chased out of the country and out of his reach enabled me to face him with all the contempt I felt for him.

No sooner had I laid down the insolent challenge than I realized those mocking words would drive him to his infamous rage, but he surprised me, answering almost silkily, "And yet, in this little jungle, as you say, the great *Capitan* Contreras does not know who you are?" His expression changed, and he straightened, his gaze swung back to the push-and-shove semblance of a line to the dilapidated station. Clearly I no longer mattered.

I turned away, but I felt him look back at me. It was strange; even though I was not looking at him, his eyes seemed to hold me in place. I could almost hear him thinking that I had not yet been dismissed. "I hardly have time for introductions, Captain, if I'm going to pack and get on that train."

With that, he set me free, turning on the heel of his shining black boots, and striding up to the station to resume his watch over the queue.

I was annoyed, perhaps even a little humiliated by his complete dismissal. The way he had stared at me, picking me apart detail by detail, had not been lascivious in the way any other soldier had looked at me during my brief stay. It was more proprietary, as he considered me property – his property – by virtue of his rank, and I held no more value to him than curiosity. I picked up my pace down the packed dirt path that served as the main road of the village. Even after all this time, my stomach turned queasily at the sight of so much poverty.

Once back in the Quonset hut that served as the Corps operations post, I began gathering my things together hastily. Unlike other Corps outposts where volunteers had their own small residences or lived with members of the community, we were newly established in this part of the country and while the populace seemed to welcome us, there was reticence about allowing us too much access to their daily lives. Therefore, for the time being at least, we were all carving space out of the Corps limited facilities.

The room was empty – hauntingly so – as I jammed clothes into one bag and medical supplies in the other. Accustomed to the twenty four hour bustle of this metal domed hospital/dining/sleeping space, I found the shallow echo of my own breathing eerie and would have welcomed any sound that would muffle it.

Almost in answer to my silent wish, I suddenly heard the rattle of machine gun fire. It wouldn't be much longer before the streets where I had been walking freely, in search of those in need, would become a battleground. I hadn't come looking for any kind of battle, even if my father was right and I had been born to fight.

I had been raised by a tough but tender ex-Marine and a lovely tomboy of a mother, both Irish Americans; my earliest recollections included the constant affirmations that I could do anything, yet I seldom had the chance. My parents had fought so many battles in their own lives that they fought twice as hard to smooth every path I might trod. I went to the best schools, knew the best people and had the best opportunities, but having everything made me yearn for a chance to earn something for myself – especially my self-respect. I decided to help people who had never had the best of anything.

So, I brought my nursing skills to a little abandoned jungle where disease was king and few people had ever seen indoor plumbing. This beautiful, multi-ethnic culture had been crushed under the heels of dictatorship for generations; a regime that stole property and discouraged education and kept its people poor and scared. As much as the conditions frightened me, I was, like every other Volunteer, challenged to improve them, and I was doing my best to make a difference here. The work was hard, sometimes we worked round the clock, but the people seemed to welcome us, cautiously. Then we started hearing whispers about a group of revolutionaries intent on overthrowing the government.

As I folded and put away those things I would not take, in the hopes that they would be found by people in need, my fingers brushed against a small Bible, printed in a Spanish/Indian dialect I did not speak, which one of my patients had presented to me as a gift. My Spanish was textbook and limited, even though we were expected to speak nothing but Spanish during our term here (how strange, then, that my conversation with Captain Contreras had been in English!) However, in this impoverish, embattled country, such a gift must have been hard to come by and I could not leave it behind. I thrust it into the pocket of my shorts as I rushed out of the abandoned hut.

The train, puffing and wheezing, was already at the station, and people were scrambling aboard: other Volunteers, US advisors and tourists, even a few locals who had scraped together enough money to bribe soldiers to look the other way, all hoping to find a space that would at least allow them to sit for the long ride to the coast. I fell into the line, such as it was, shifting the weight of my bags from hand to the other, just as I shifted arguments for and against staying behind. I loathed the idea of scampering out like a whipped puppy, just when I was learning how to fight, but nothing in my twenty five years had prepared me for facing a war – even though I knew that's when a nurse would be needed most.

There was shouting behind us, and most of us turned to look, but no one was compelled to help the heavily pregnant woman being pushed around by so many soldiers. My blood boiled at the lewd and threatening remarks the soldiers made (for I had learned Spanish profanity in abundance) as they grabbed at the girl with the swollen belly and frightened face. She couldn't have even been my age.

"Stop it!" I shouted, dropping my larger bag and losing my place in the queue, as I rushed out to shield the girl from further harassment. "Leave her alone," I demanded, swinging my smaller bag like a weapon against the soldiers as I put myself between them and their target.

I understood the filthy comments they made about us – abuse is abuse in any language. "Just get away from here, you pigs! You animals don't know how to treat human beings because you don't know what it means to be one." I pulled my arms around the trembling girl. "Shh, shh, it's all right."

The girl's ash colored face and dull eyes worried me and I suspected there was something wrong with the pregnancy. *"¿El bebé viene pronto?"* I asked.

Again the soldiers began jeering and laughing, suggesting that it should be born dead, as it deserved. "Shut your filthy mouths!" I shouted and the gathering soldiers stepped back in surprise. To tell the truth, I was surprised, too. I turned to the girl. "Go home," I ordered the girl. "Run while you still can." I stayed between her and the soldiers.

"It does not matter to us," one soldier leered as they began to advance again. "One woman is much like another to us." He caught my arm and pulled me into the closing circle. "With you, no fat belly gets in the way." He patted my flat stomach.

"*Déjame ir ahora*." I commanded. "Let me go. Help me!" I called out to the passengers climbing onto the train, but they only looked on as I was dragged away. The train answered with a whistle and a rattle and a cloud of steam and it began to pull away from the station. "The train!" I shouted stupidly, as if these soldiers would actually take a train schedule into consideration when considering rape.

Other soldiers, with leering smiles and dirty uniforms began to press in on all sides, touching me, trying to kiss me, laughing at my furious but puny attempts to extricate myself. "I'm going to be sick," I moaned as one of the more repulsive creatures managed to work his hand underneath my shirt, but that only made them all laugh louder.

As they began to pull me in the direction of an alley behind the station, a lone figure eased himself away from the shadows of a building and approached them. I recognized his cold, insolently amused stare even from my precarious vantage point, being carried along, upright among them, my feet dangling above the dirt street, kicking uselessly as I struggled. Oh, no, I prayed, not him, too.

The others saw his approach and called out to him jovially, as if offering to share a bottle of wine instead of a human being. I watched, horrified, as he closed in, the crowd falling aside to let him near, finally letting my feet touch ground, as I was suddenly alone, in the circle, and the arrogant Captain Contreres stood before me. "So," he said, his hands on his hips, his feet set apart, his posture one of absolute command.

I looked up at him, determined not to give in without a far bigger battle than he anticipated. "We meet again, Captain," I answered in English, matching his haughty tone.

He looked at me for a moment, and if he was surprised by my response, he hid it well. "You have done a foolish thing, *Senorita*," he told me, gravely. "Now your escape route is gone and you are in peril." He gestured dramatically toward the last visible puff of steam from the ancient train.

I squared my shoulders and lifted my chin. "No more than you, Captain," I answered far more bravely than I had a right to do. "I'm not just an American citizen, I'm a Peace Corps Volunteer. You'll be held accountable if anything happens to me."

A hush fell around us. They might not have understood our words, but they could see that what I had said had some impact on the great and powerful *Capitan* Contreras.

"That is so," he acknowledged, nodding curtly, even as his black eyes slid over me. It wasn't an admiring gaze, it was that same proprietary look he had given me before. I almost wished there was some modicum of admiration there. I was used to that, even at home in America, but I had never had any desire to exploit or be exploited by my appeal to men. I continued to meet his gaze evenly. I wasn't yet ready to surrender.

He did not seem prepared to do battle then, either, for he sighed heavily. "Very well." He barked an order and everyone around them stepped back a little more and an opening appeared in the group. "Come this way."

A rumble of protest rippled through the men as I straightened my shirt and retraced their steps to collect my bags. The protest was quelled by one swift, sharp look from the man who had demanded my release. "My office is this way," he directed. He ignored the opportunity to show some courtesy by assisting me with my bags, but, in truth, I would have been astounded if he had taken one or both. Women in this country were meant to be beasts of burden, not men.

I didn't waste any time being grateful for his intervention. I knew exactly what was on the captain's agenda. "If you were a gentleman," I grumbled, "you'd help me with these."

He looked over his shoulder at me, a brow arched in surprise. "If I were a gentleman," he agreed, tightly, "I would be dead."

I snorted derisively. "Am I supposed to see that as an improvement?"

He stopped, glaring down at me. "You will hold your tongue in my presence," he demanded.

"Then I'll endeavor to stay out of your presence," I returned sharply. I wasn't exactly resigned to my fate, but I saw no reason to go meekly toward the inevitable, either. After all, the train was gone, I was under his control, in all likelihood I would be raped and killed, how much greater would my danger be for speaking my mind? For a moment, I considered running...but where would I go? I was in an open square with angry soldiers at the other end. There was no place I could go, and even if I could get out of the open and into some hiding place, how long could I survive? So, I followed him, juggling luggage and fears.

"That, I'm afraid," he returned finally, "is impossible, *Senorita*."

"What? You afraid? *That* is impossible."

"You try me," he warned, looking sternly in my direction. "No wonder American men are so soft. They fetch and carry for their women and allow them to be disrespectful."

"I don't know about that," I grunted, shifting the heavier bag to my other hand. "No man's ever given me a reason to be disrespectful...until now." The strap of the smaller bag slipped from my shoulder and I scrambled for it.

He sighed in exasperation as I paused to readjust it. Flicking a glance back to the town square, he saw that his company had dispersed, and there wasn't much chance of anyone witnessing what he did next. "Give that to me." He snatched the hand of the suitcase from my hand.

"Thank you," I murmured, astounded.

"*De nada*," he answered, and added impatiently, "Do not become accustomed to such service. It is not," he paused to indicate a door, "part of the accommodations."

"I shall try not to," I paused to look up at a large white structure. I'd been past the building many times. I had always been startled by the stark difference between the humble thatched roofed, mud walled houses and this significant two storey building. I swallowed and began again. "I shall try not to become accustomed to anything about you."

"*Por Dios*," he spat, rolling his eyes Heavenward. "You must be in need of a beating." He stepped up and yanked open the door.

I glanced up and down the street. If I ran, he would shoot me. There really was nowhere else to go. As long as I was alive, I might still find a way to escape. I followed him to the threshold and stalled.

The foyer was immense, with two staircases, a brightly painted domed ceiling, and half dozen doors visible on each level. I was not unaccustomed to such opulence – my family home was similar in size and grandeur – but here, such a place seemed more than out of place. It seemed obscene.

He had put down my bag and opened a door nearby. Realizing that I had not followed him, he turned and frowned at me. "What are you looking at?"

"How many people live here?" I asked. "Thirty people could live here."

"It is large," he agreed, gesturing for me to come into the room he had opened, "but I like the space."

"Do you mean it is for you alone?"

"For me?" he echoed. "No, for the Army. It is our headquarters, but I sleep here."

I continued to stare. Ever since the first time I had seen this building I had been imagining what a magnificent hospital it would be, and to learn that he kept it for himself infuriated me beyond words.

"*Senorita*," he complained, "come in and shut the door. There could be snipers anywhere."

"How dare you!" I cried, spurred to speech at last. I crossed the threshold, the elegant tiles of the foyer and to the door where he waited. "How dare you?"

He reacted in surprise. “Now what have I done?”

“How dare you live in all this glory and comfort when from every window of this place you can watch children die of filth, disease and hunger?” I wanted to kick him, slap him, pummel him with my fists, but I stood there, motionless except for the tremble of rage.

He shrugged, negligently. “They do not concern me,” he answered, flicking the subject away as if it were no more than a pesky bug. “They are not my responsibility or my duty. My duty is to put down an insurrection. If they are they to be raised as rebellious to authority, then it is better that they die young.”

“’Better’?” I repeated, feeling nauseated by his words. “They are human beings, Captain.”

“That, *Senorita,* is a matter of opinion.” He gestured for me to enter the room.

“You arrogant pig. You disgust me the way you walk around as if you were a…a king with a crown of green,” I gestured toward the green, billed military cap, “adorned with the witness of your bravery.” I jabbed at one of the brightly colored medals over his heart. “Some bravery: shooting unarmed children.”

He ignored my words, staring at me in fascination. I suppose he had never been addressed by a woman in any form, and certainly not with the fierce condemnation I was laying at his door, and the novelty of it overshadowed any indignation he might feel. He continued to stare at me, even after I finished speaking, until a sharp snap sound to his right. It might have been a breaking twig or the cocking of a gun that broke his reverie and he caught my hand and dragged me behind the door. "Sit down and be still, *nina*," he told me, flinging me into a chair.

"Don't push me around," I began, trying to stand, but he forced me back into the chair with a bone crushing grip.

He was smiling at me, taking pleasure in what he perceived as my meek submission but, save a small wince of pain, I continued to glare at him. "I said," he repeated in a cold, low voice, "be still." He moved to a window adorned with thick, dark curtains, and cautiously pulled one aside enough to look outside. He repeated the action at another window, and finally, satisfied, settled in a chair and laced his fingers over his chest as he smiled, meanly, at me.

"What do you think you are going to do with me?" I demanded.

"Do not ask questions."

"I have a right to-"

"You have no rights," he told me, bluntly. "You will stay alive on my sufferance only. I acknowledge the political expedience of keeping you alive, but at any time inconvenience outweighs expedience, I'll eliminate you personally. If and until that time, you will do what I say, when I say, and you will ask me no questions." He punctuated each statement with the ticking off of long, lean brown fingers.

"In other words, you intend to treat me as if I were one of those-" I flicked a hand toward the window, "so called rebels."

He said a word that was beyond my study of the language. "You are more trouble than all those rebels," he spat, slapping the top of the huge ebony desk beside his chair. "At least they respect the crack of the whip. You will have to be taught."

Fury flashed through me. I jumped to my feet even before the idea had formed in my mind. "Then shoot me now."

He glanced at the window and then at me. "Will you sit down?" he said icily. "And no more of this schoolgirl melodrama."

"Captain Contreras," I said with equal coldness, even though I was white hot with rage inside, "I come from a country where we prize freedom and human rights over life itself. Without either, I have no life. Just shoot me now, because if you lay one finger on me in violence or subjugation, I will fight you to the death."

His chin dropped open, and he stared at me as if I'd grown another head. "Will you please sit down?" he asked in a softer voice. "And let us have no more talk of shooting. It is too tempting. What am I to do with you? The Americans and the… then…" he snapped his fingers, expecting me to supply the words he lacked.

"Peace Corps."

"The Americans and the Peace Corps will want to know why I am holding you hostage. I will have to prove that I will be responsible for your safety." He rubbed his temple, as if his head ached. "I should have put you on that train myself."

I sat again, slowly, in a discomfort more basic than fear. "Captain," I began.

"Hush, *Senorita-*" he stopped and looked me over again. "It is *Senorita*?"

"Yes."

He waited.

I watched him.

He sighed again. "You do have a name, do you not?"

"McKee," I told him stiffly. "Dinah McKee." If I had a rank and serial number, I would have gladly given him those, as well.

"Dinah McKee." He seemed to be savoring the name. "What compelled you to come down here and interfere in what is none of your business?"

"It's where the Peace Corps sent me," I explained.

He shook his head, as if he didn't believe he had heard correctly. "You speak with education, your manner is one of breeding, your skin, clothing, hair all indicate affluent upbringing – even your Spanish, while too formal to be native, is clear and comprehendible. With all that to commend you, you felt your only option was the Peace Corps? Why?"

"Money," I answered baldly. "My parents, as you surmised, are well off and they bought me everything I ever wanted. I wanted a chance to earn my own way for a change." I'm not sure why I let my story spill out so easily; surely he wouldn't care how I felt, but the words just kept coming. "I wanted to help those less fortunate and I am a nurse, so-"

"You are a nurse?" he repeated in the tone of a clerk wearily filling in a form, but I could see a veritable computing machine at work behind those black eyes, and I knew nothing I said to him would ever be forgotten. "Interesting."

The discomfort was growing worse. "Yes. Captain, I—"

"Shh, I am thinking." He closed his eyes.

"Captain," I persisted, "if you don't tell me where I can find a bathroom, you're going to be very sorry."

His eyes flew open and his expression was one of horror. He pointed, struggling for words. It would have been funny if my needs had not been so acute. As I stood and hurried toward the door indicated, he called after me, "I'm watching the patio. If you try to escape, I will come after you, and I will rethink the idea of shooting you."

I ignored him and pulled open the door, letting it slam behind me.

As I was washing my hands, I heard the clatter of boots on the stone patio outside – one of the men coming to report, no doubt. I stepped to the door, holding my breath.

"*Capitan,*" the soldier addressed him. I could a rustle that sounded like a smart salute.

"Juarez," he answered irritably.

"There is a report of rebels waiting for the cover of dark to take this headquarters by force. They have acquired several automatic weapons."

How did you learn this?" The captain didn't sound at all concerned by this news. He didn't even sound interested.

"We were able to make one of them talk. She did not wish to talk at first, but she was...persuaded."

It took me a moment to understand what he had said, but when the full meaning came to me, I gasped. Hands clapped over my mouth, I backed away from the door.

I heard steps coming toward the door and the captain's voice was nearer now. "We will be ready."

"*Capitan*? The other girl...the one with the white hair..."

"Forget her," the captain barked. He was very close to the door now.

"But, *Capitan*, the men-"

"I said forget her. She is American. We cannot afford to-"

"Who would know?" There was slime in his voice. I felt dirty just listening. "And why should we be so careful? Everyone knows the Americans are providing the weapons for these rebels."

"Everyone?" I heard the captain turn around. "How is it everyone knows when I do not know? Go. As for the woman...we'll discuss her later... when I am through with her."

I swallowed hard, eyes fixed on the door handle. Outside the door, I heard a deep sigh, and then the latch lifted and the door opened. He looked at me, and then over his shoulder. "Come, *Senorita,*" he instructed in English. Before I could resist, he caught my arm and pulled me through the door and up the stairs.

This is it, I thought, feeling my throat constrict in fear, and my mouth go dry. For several nights I had listened to the sporadic machine gun fire out in the jungle beyond our headquarters and now I was looking a human machine gun in the eyes. The words of his soldier, which boasted of his brutality echoed round and round in my ears, chased by the captain's casually given promise. Now he led me upstairs to where, undoubtedly, a bed waited, and in that bed was a new unknown. Somehow I had to reach any spark of compassion in this heartless man, and make him realize just how unknown it would be. "*Senor*," I began, almost pleading. "I am-"

"I know you are an American," he interrupted gruffly. "Because of that, I will take you to the coast tomorrow. But, you must stay here tonight." We had reached the landing and he pushed me toward a door on the left.

I froze. "I can't."

He looked at me. He seemed puzzled by my fear, and the strident tone of my voice. Below us we could hear the click click click of boots in the hallway. "You have no choice," he informed me in a low voice. "Either you stay here, under my protection, or you will be caught again by my men and they will-"

"I know what they'll do," I answered with a shudder. I'd seen enough of their handiwork already, so I followed him obediently through the door.

I found myself in a cavernous bedroom, larger than any I'd ever seen, and appointed with all would expect from such a man. "Stay here," he said.

I looked around, nothing the masculine details, the dark wood, the sturdy yet elegant furniture, the rich colors, and the undeniable stamp of Captain Contreras. "This is your room, isn't it?"

He shrugged and opened the door to depart. "Where else would I put the woman I am sleeping with tonight?" I flinched at his words, and he pulled back into the room. "No one will disturb you here."

The look in his eyes seemed to be re-assuring; all he was offering me was sanctuary and tomorrow it would be all over. I wanted to thank him, but my voice refused to function and my jaw worked soundlessly. I nodded, instead.

"I will bring you something to eat," he offered, looking as uncomfortable as I felt. Clearly, being accommodating to a woman was outside his experience.

"No, thank you," I managed to mumble. My head didn't seem to be working right, either. Suddenly the light seemed to be all around me at odd angles and nothing seemed to be standing straight. My fingers curled around the ornately carved bedpost, and I felt as if I were clinging for my life. At that precise moment, I could not explain where I was or how I got there, or why I wasn't at home on the hill looking down on Pontchartrain.

"You look unwell," he said, coming toward me, but hesitating a few steps away. "You...have had an upsetting day." He fumbled with the bed-clothes, and drew back a heavy red and gold cover. "You should rest."

I had enough awareness to draw back when he came near the bed, and a little more to scold myself for the childish reaction. "No, I'm all right," I lied. "Why wouldn't my eyes work properly? Why couldn't they focus on anything but that bed? Why was I hot, then cold, then hot again? Why did the laughter coming up from the courtyard put my teeth on edge and make me want to scream? Was this fear? I'd never known anything like it before.

His face had darkened angrily. "Must I put you there myself?" he demanded.

"No, really, I'm quite…"

I'm not sure what happened, but one moment I was insisting I was well enough to look after myself, and the next I was in the bed and he was removing my shoes. "Rest, Dinah McKee," he said in an unexpectedly gentle whisper. "Rest and pray tomorrow comes quickly."

I opened my eyes, turning my face toward his voice. He was looking down at me with the most peculiar expression, and I realized that he had wound one lock of my hair around his finger. "For," he continued, easing his hand away, "I do not promise that your rest will be undisturbed."

A violent shudder raced through me. *I should pray tomorrow comes quickly*, I thought, feeling faint again, *or not at all.*

Chapter Two
The Captain

Darkness had fallen, sending shadows across the fine appointments of the room, and the air was strangely still for a night filled with so much potential for violence, and sweet with the fragrance of night blooming flowers in the garden below. Yet, I couldn't rest. My dreams had been wild, desperate and undefinable, forcing me awake and making my heart pound. I had head the words of the soldier, Juarez, reporting to the captain, and I waited, on edge for the first sounds of battle, the first cries of pain, of outrage, of protest, of victory and of death. The downtrodden, victimized people of this country were rising up, and if the soldier's information was to be believed, some outside source was supplying the people with a more level battlefield. More weapons only meant more bloodshed. I would be needed, but I was being held here, in this palace, my safety hinged on one man's sobriety and sufferance. The stillness was suffocating me.

I sat up, throwing the heavy bedclothes back, and swung my legs over the side of the bed.

Outside, coarse laughter exploded, making me jump. Picking up my shoes, I crept to the door, wondering if I could escape in the confusion of the first attack.

There were heavy footsteps in the hall beyond the door, causing me to scurry back to the bed. Had he changed his mind? Had the soldiers overpowered him? Had the rebels overtaken the headquarters? My eyes locked on the door handle in dread. Who would come through that door?

It was the captain. In one hand he balanced a silver tray, with a covered dish and crystal decanter filled with amber liquid. He almost smiled as he put the tray down on a table nearby. "I am surprised you did not attempt to lock the door," he observed.

I looked past him. "It is a very beautiful a door," I answered, allowing him to infer what he liked from my observation.

He smiled. I knew he inferred exactly what I meant. "I brought you some food." He gestured toward the tray. "With all that has happened today, it's unlikely you've had a chance to eat."

"Thank you, but no thank you." Even though I was fully dressed, the way he was looking at me made me want to pull all the bedclothes around me, as if I were naked.

"You should eat, *Senorita*. You'll need your strength." He lifted the lid of the covered dish and an unexpectedly pleasant aroma wafted toward me. It appeared to be a rice dish, made golden by some heavenly spice. "Surely, as a nurse, you know how important it is to nourish the body." He put the lid to one side and lifted the decanter, filling two glasses. "Also, it is quite delicious." He handed one glass to me, and retained the other as he settled into a large chair not far from the bed.

"I feel like the calf being fattened for the sacrifice," I muttered as another raucous laugh exploded outside.

He raised his head to listen. "Pay no attention to them," he advised. "They are soldiers, with a greater passion for blood than for lust. They are preparing for the battle, so a mere woman will soon be forgotten." He forked up some of the food and offered it to me. "So, now you will eat."

I opened my mouth slowly, like a recalcitrant child forced into eating my vegetables.

He observed my expression with amusement. "You think perhaps I would poison you?" he suggested.

I swallowed the food without tasting it. "Now that you mention it."

He took a bite for himself. "Nonsense." He savored and swallowed. "You see?"

I took a sip from the glass he had filled for me. Feeling his eyes fixed on me for some reaction, I allowed, "It's good."

He shifted upward in his chair. It was the first time I had ever seen someone embody the expression 'puffed up with pride.' "Napoleon Brandy," he told me. "I am not so barbaric as you think."

I put the glass down. "Napoleon Brandy does not make you any more civilized in my eyes," I retorted. "The money you spent on this bottle could have bought food and clothing for a dozen children."

He spoke through gritted teeth. "You try my patience. What is your concern with people who are beneath you?" He pointed at me. "Which are less than the dust under my feet?"

"Surely the great *Capitan* Contreras would not allow his feet to touch dust," I observed in mock horror.

He sat forward, hand raised to slap me.

"Go ahead," I told him coldly. "Slap me. Beat me. It cannot lower my opinion of you any further."

He sat back, swearing under his breath. "Your father should have beaten you from the cradle."

Relief cooled the heat in my face, but I couldn't let him see that I had actually feared his actions. "Your father should have done the same," I retorted.

"Have you no fear, woman? I could snuff out your life...like...like..." he slapped the arm of his chair. "Like that, and take much pleasure in it."

"Perhaps," I agreed evenly, despite the chill that rippled down my spine, "but it would take all of your weapons and brute strength to do so." I pushed the plate away. "Frankly, life under your 'sufferance' really isn't a life at all." The voice I heard coming out of my mouth sounded nothing like the very frightened girl inside, but I could not let him see fear. Fear would only feed his power. He might destroy me, but I intended to stain his memory for it.

He sat back, hands curled over the ends of the chair arms, watching me as if he suspected my calm was just a façade and would crack under his scrutiny. "Tell me about yourself, *nina*," he said, at last. "What sort of home do you come from that gives you the roar of a lion in the body of a gazelle?"

"A good home," I answered with an unexpected pang of homesickness. I was never going to see my parents again.

"No doubt." He shifted around to use one fist as a pedestal for his square chin. "What part of your country?"

"New Orleans. That's in Louisiana, on the Gulf Coast." At that moment, I could almost hear street corner jazz and smell beignets from a *boulangerie*. To the rest of the world my home town meant Mardi Gras and riotous behavior, but to me it was simply the best home in the world.

"Ah, that explains the..." he paused to search for a word, "swing in your speech. I have heard many Americans speak, and you do not sound like any I've heard. I like it," he added after a moment. "It's not so harsh as some." He leaned forward and pushed the plate toward me again. "Go on. Eat and tell me more."

"Well..." I eyed the plate hungrily. "I don't know what else to tell you. My parents made sure I had a good education, and a broad understanding of the world, and made me aware of the needs of others. I decided I wanted to help others so, when I finished nursing school, I volunteered for a rotating clinic service which went into the bayou to help people who didn't have much access to medical care."

He leaned forward again, giving the plate another nearly imperceptible nudge toward me. "It seems like a dangerous endeavor."

I gave in and reached for the fork. "There were some frightening moments, but I don't scare off easily, and I really enjoyed seeing the changes – even little ones – that I could make." I reached for my glass. "Even in America, little children can die of starvation and neglect. It's a hideous situation." I put the glass down and took another bite. "Then one day I heard about the good things the Peace Corps was doing in third world countries. I had to join. They sent me here."

He seemed mystified, shaking his head, slowly. “And your father did not prevent it? If I had a daughter, she would be sheltered and groomed for her husband and the children she would bear.”

I made a face at the idea. “My father’s not like that, thank goodness.”

“You are very brave – for a woman,” he allowed. His tone suggested that he thought he was bestowing a great compliment.

“My father and mother knew I had to go where my heart told me I could help. I am not inclined to sit at home waiting for a man and child.”

“Oh?” That astounded him. His dark brows nearly disappeared beneath the wave of jet black hair across his forehead. “You do not want children?”

“Someday, I suppose.” I put the fork down. “I have too much to do right now, though, to settle down and please the whims of one man.”

He let his eyes slide over me in an unmistakably meaningful manner. “I would image that you are most adept at it, when you try.”

I felt the color rush back to my face as I struggled with embarrassment and rage. “I don’t intend to show you.”

Those dark eyes hardened for a moment. “I think, if the time allowed, I would let you recant that statement,” he told me, insolently. “But, as it is, I have work of my own to do.” He levered himself out of the chair with his powerful forearms and looked over his shoulder at my two cases, which, at some point had appeared in the room, though I do not remember him bringing them up. "Pack all that you must have in that smaller bag. I plan to move once darkness is full and I cannot be waiting for you to drag everything along."

"Where are we going?" I pushed the tray aside and slid to the floor.

"My reconnaissance tells me there is already some fighting to the north," he murmured, frowning. "We will deploy our troops there tonight – my men are waiting for me to lead them."

More laughter rang out below us, as if on cue. "Those men?" I asked, alarmed.

He waved my concern away. "These few men will stay here and protect the headquarters while we-" he gestured to include me, "go north, under cover of darkness. Once I have accessed the situation, I will take you to the coast. Your Marines have ships off the coast, and one of them will take you home." He met my eyes for the first time. "It will be a dangerous journey, and you must be as brave and strong as you have been so far, *Senorita* McKee. But," he paused, waiting for the loud laughter from below to subside, "I cannot leave you behind."

For that I had to be grateful. "Thank you."

"Now, eat." He pointed at the tray again. "Who knows when you'll have another chance."

I couldn't argue with that. "Very well. " I reached for the plate. It was a good thing I came from pragmatic stock. My life hinged on his admiration of my spirit and strength. "When do we leave?"

He had turned toward the window, looking down at the gathering of men on the patio below. "In an hour, perhaps." He frowned. "*Senorita*. Dinah." He turned around sharply. "Remove your..." he gestured as sharply as he spoke, "*camisa*."

I stared at him, horrified and betrayed. "What?" Oh, surely not now!

"Do not argue." He moved across the room, tugging at his own uniform. "Listen," he hissed.

I could hear the shouting from outside and the footsteps rapping up the tile steps. My nerveless fingers struggled with the buttons of my blouse as he put the tray of food on the table near the door and threw his shirt on the floor. I held out my shirt, nervously.

"And that, too." He pointed to the strap of my bra.

I cringed from his assessing stare, but I obeyed, tugging up the bedclothes to cover myself.

He dropped my bra on the floor, as well, on his way to the door. He listened for a moment, then ever so carefully flicked the lock into place. "Get into the bed," he commanded, dragging his hands through his hair. "We have no time to delay. He jerked the blankets and sheets out of my hands and pushed me backward into the pillows before dragging the quilt up over me. “It would not hurt for you to *look* frightened now.”

That was certainly no challenge. I knew I was almost in tears; I was confused and frightened and had no clue what was going to happen next.

The door was tried furtively.

He looked at me, with a finger to his lips. Now I understood.

After a moment, there was a sharp knock on the door. “*¿Quién es*?” he called, making a great show of throwing back the bedclothes on the opposite side of the bed.

“Juarez, *Capitan*.” I recognized the voice and shivered; it evoked images of cruelty. He spoke in choppy English, which surprised me. “The rebels are moving in from the south. “They will be here by nightfall.”

The captain crossed the room and pulled open the door. Juarez’ face appeared, taking the scene with frank curiosity. His eyes fell on me, huddling under the bedclothes and that sadistic grin I’d seen before spread across his face. I felt like a meaty bone before a starving dog. “You will need to leave soon,” he continued, still looking at me.

The captain murmured something and Juarez’ grin faltered, but he continued to look at me. “The girl…”

"I will be down shortly," the captain barked. He bent over and picked up my shirt and bra. "Dress yourself," he commanded. "We will finish this later."

"But, *Capitan*," Juarez protested.

I could not see the expression on the Captain's face, but he could, and it must have been lethal. He stumbled back a step, his eyes dropping to the ground. "I will be going into battle, too," the captain continued coldly, "and perhaps to my death. I did not spend last night...interrogating a woman from the village. Are you going to suggest you have more right to this," he waved toward me, "than I?" He kicked the door shut and leaned against it, eyes shut tight. "Gather your things," he said, tersely. "We are going to leave sooner than planned." His eyes scanned the floor and focused on something. He stooped and collected the little Bible that had fallen from my pocket, and he thumbed through it briefly before leaving it on the bed.

I continued to hold the quilt up, covering myself, as I watched him. The little vignette had been a brilliant move on his part. "No wonder you are a captain," I whispered.

He turned as if to confirm that I had spoken, and bowed slightly. "*Gracias.* Now, dress yourself, or I will be forced to take you out just as you are." He lifted my bags to the bed and tugged them open.

My fingers tightened around the edges of the quilt. "Go," I implored. "I can't dress with you watching."

"You took the things off quick enough," he pointed out.

"Yes, but there was no time to think about it, then," I protested. "Now I have time to think about it and I can't."

He sighed and made an elaborate show of turning his back. "Will this do?"

I snatched up my bra and fastened it. He turned again as I was shrugging into my blouse. "Now, pack quickly. We must be away from here before anyone realizes we have gone." He marched to a cabinet at the far side of the room. From it, he took two guns and several boxes of ammunition. Aware of my alarmed expression, he looked up. "You did not expect me to pack for a picnic, did you?" he mocked.

I shook my head. I had honestly come to this country believing I understood the reality of it, but until I watched him methodically packing up his weaponry I had not understood it at all.

After a moment, he pursed his lips and reached into the cabinet again. "Can you shoot, Dinah?"

"My father taught me how to handle guns when I was younger," I admitted. "He thought I should know." I didn't add that I loathed any method of violence – especially guns. They struck me as cowardly. One could maim or kill people without even revealing one's self or meeting the eyes of one's victim.

"He was a wise man." He strode toward the bed and held something out to me. It was a small, silvery pistol. "Take it. It may become necessary to defend yourself."

I stared at him, horrified, but I took it, holding it gingerly as it if were on fire, and put it into the bag I had been filling with as much as I dared: medical supplies, comb and brush, toothbrush, soap, a change of underwear, and that gun. On top I placed the small Bible and the picture of my family. "Aren't you afraid I'll shoot you and escape?" I asked, taking the bullets he offered me, as well.

"No." He actually smiled at me and it seemed to transform his harsh face. "You are many annoying things, *Senorita*, but you are not a fool. I am your only hope for freedom, now and you know it. You will not shoot me." He reached into the bag and rummaged. "You are an extraordinary female," he said with an odd touch of warmth as he replaced the photo of David, my father, Janice, my mother and Duncan, my cat. "You would have made an excellent man."

"I assume, from your point of view that is a compliment," I observed tightly, pulling the bag shut. "What do you mean?"

"You pack with such practicality. You leave behind the very things that most women consider necessary: the cosmetics, the jewelry and perfume and take medical supplies and a gun." He turned his hand over. "That's the mind of a good man. And there are not even many of those."

"I agree," I muttered.

He stiffened and reined in anger with effort. "Shall we go?"

I nodded and let him guide me, his hand resting against my arm.

We slipped out through a window, to a narrow ledge that led to the back of the house, where we slid down column, and into the shadows of a large tree. He indicated that I should wait there and, watching left and right, darted across the long back porch and inside. I crouched beneath oleander bushes, listening to the conversations and laughter coming from the terrace on the other side of the house. I was beginning to think he had left me there to be captured, or he had been captured himself, when finally the door pushed open and he slipped out, a canvas bag slung over his shoulder. He did not creep toward me, but he did walk warily, one hand on the grip of the gun at his side.

Ducking into the bushes, he put the bag down in front of me, indicating that I should look inside. He had packed a picnic after all. The bag bulged with food and a canvas covered canteen of brandy. It was not gourmet ingredients that he had jammed into the bag, but common sense staples of survival. Only the brandy seemed in keeping with his characteristic demand for the best.

He stood again, shouldered the bag and reached for my hand, pulling me upright sharply, and holding me back as he drew his gun and looked slowly from right to left and back again. “This way,” he whispered, releasing my hand to point across a small patch of lawn which faded into a dense outcropping of trees. To my surprise, he wrapped his arm around me, pulling me hard against him as if to shield me from bullets as we hurried across the open space.

Once under the cover of the trees he allowed me to ease away, but did not let go of me entirely. He walked quickly and I stumbled along behind him. I wondered if he knew where we were going as we went deeper and deeper into the jungle which refused to be held back by the village. We seemed to be moving, at least in my case, with a dizzying need to be anywhere but where we had been.

We moved at this pace for a long time, until I just knew my next step would be my last. He stopped suddenly, and held me up against him as I gasped and gulped breath that burned my lungs. “Listen,” he whispered harshly, pushing me back against a tree.

From the direction we'd come, I could hear the horrible popping of gunfire. Television and movies have got it all wrong, I had learned. It isn't all bangs and rat-tat-tat; it is hisses and pops and thuds.

And screams. I could hear horrible battle cries, and the wails of grief and pain, even over the distance we had already covered. I moaned and twisted toward the tree, clinging to it for support.

"We cannot linger," he told me, brusquely, pulling at my shoulder, as I struggled to hide my sobs. "We will be missed soon – either by my men or by those who will attack. In either case, there will be a search. We must keep moving, but we will not run anymore." He slid his hand down my arm to my wrist and begin to tug.

As the brush became more and more dense, our progress slowed. We both walked, watching for predators of any kind, without conversation, and as the hours passed I became tuned to his movements. I knew when he was going to stop and listen intently. I knew not to speak or move when he paused, and I learned not to bump into him, either.

I marched along silently, swatting at flies, as if in a trance, my mind whirling with a montage of images: faces flashing with pain and rage and hatred and fear, and beyond them all, I saw an enormous maw of uncertainty opened up, ready to swallow us all.

We came across a small stream along our path, and there he paused and lowered himself to a fallen log. "Sit," he whispered.

I sat and he opened the canteen and raised it to his lips. I watched him, thirstily. The canteen hovered over his mouth and he lowered it and offered it to me. "Drink," he instructed, "but, only a little. We still have a long way to go."

I took a sip, gratefully, and let the burning smoothness fall down my throat. "Thank you." I held it out to him and watched him tilt it toward his own lips.

"We cannot sit too long," he told me as he screwed the cap back on. "There is another village near here - on that road," he pointed, "that we travel alongside. And there may be people yet there, watching for us."

"Is that why we're not travelling on the road itself?"

"*Si.*" He turned in the half light of moonshine, through the thick leaves. "How do you do?"

It took a moment to understand what he was asking. "I'll make it," I said with more confidence than I felt. I rubbed my weary legs and tried to stand.

He patted one of them, keeping me in place. "I know you will, Dinah McKee. You have good instincts for survival, though I do not understand how or why." He shook his head.

"In my country, freedom is worth fighting for, Captain-"

"Call me Javier," he invited, his fingers kneading my leg.

I jerked away. "Shouldn't we be going, Captain?"

He set mouth angrily. "*Si, vamonos.*"

I stood and followed him. As we reached the turn off the path that brought us near the village he had mentioned, I could hear the low moans of someone in pain. I moved in the direction of the sounds, but his strong hand came down on my shoulder, roughly. "Where are you going?" he hissed.

"Someone is in pain," I answered, trying to shrug his hand away. "I'm a nurse, it's my duty to-"

"Did it not occur to you that it may be a trap?" he suggested harshly. "Or is it your duty to get yourself killed?"

"Captain, are you not willing to give your life for this cause?" I responded, digging into my bag.

He straightened, proudly. "It is my cause."

"Well, easing human suffering is my cause." I straightened, too - with the gun in my hand. "Now, let go of me."

His black gaze jerked to my hand and back to my eyes. "You intend to shoot me?" he asked in an incredulous voice.

I was startled by the question, and I looked down to the gun in my hand. "No, I intend to protect myself, in case it is a trap," I answered hotly. "But, I will shoot you if you don't let go of me."

His hand fell away from mine.

I moved and he followed. "What are you doing?" I whispered over my shoulder.

"Going with you."

"Stay here," I insisted. "I'll be right back." With a deep breath, I began to move toward the sounds of pain, the gun tucked into the waistband of my shorts, just as I had seen done in movies.

"Dinah-"

I turned that superior smile he used so often back on him. "Do you really think I'd choose this time and place to escape? I'm just going to see who needs my help."

He opened his mouth to argue, and surrendered with a groan. Sinking to the log, he gestured toward the road. "Go with God."

What a puzzle, I thought, moving forward cautiously.

The village he spoke of was nothing more than a few huts crowded around a slimy looking well. The street was merely dirt cleared of underbrush and beaten down by the feet of people moving through on their way to someplace else. The jungle hovered all around, night animals making enough sound to remind man that they still dominated the land and had only allowed them this little space for their pitiful attempts at farming and a few mean shelters.

The moans were louder now, as if the pain was increasing. I listened to them, shivering, reminded more of a wounded animal than a human being. Another sound came – a shriek of protest that jerked me forward, running heedless of any trap, toward the last house on the road.

Bursting through the ragged cloth curtain that served as a door, I found the woman I'd tried to rescue the day before. She was sprawled on a filthy straw mat, obviously in labor and in great pain. Her tears made muddy streaks down her face, and her long, tangled hair swished back and forth on the dirt floor as she clutched her belly and rocked with her legs.

For the moment, I had forgotten that I was now running for my life in a world on the brink of war. I knelt before the woman, murmuring in the most soothing tone I could manage, while I tried to get her into a position where I could examine her. The baby was already well into the birth canal, but he was presenting breech and it was too late for any intervention I could make on my own.

The poor girl didn't look strong enough to survive such a delivery. She looked so young, and she was very thin. She also looked as if she had been beaten recently – there were deep purple marks on her cheek, her shoulder and her thigh.

I could feel the sting of helpless tears and I blinked them away. I couldn't let her see how hopeless the situation was. All my education and all my practical training seemed wasted at that moment and, above all other things, I hate waste. At that moment, I also hated the *junta* responsible for this.

There was a rustle of stealthy steps outside and I reached for the gun almost before I realized what I was doing. I knew the girl's condition was by no means contrived, but that did not necessarily guarantee that we were the only two left in the village. Inching back against the wall, I waited, holding my breath, grateful that my patient was in no condition to cry out a warning or anything more than a few pitiful prayers.

The steps slowed just outside the hut and I eased the gun free and aimed it at the top of the door. I wished I could see better, but there was no other opening in the room to let in moonlight in.

The cloth flap was pushed back abruptly. The captain's head appeared, the barrel of his gun lifted even with his cheek, his shiny, black eyes darting around to take in every detail. Seeing me crouched on the floor, my gun poised to shoot, he lowered his own weapon and demanded, "Well?"

I sagged against the wall in a rush of relief. "It's you." The girl on the floor reacted to his appearance by whimpering and trying to crawl away. I had to reach for her and hold her still. "Thank God you're here. The baby is coming breech. I need your help."

He surveyed the situation. "My help?" he repeated, scowling at the figure on the floor as if she were some repulsive insect.

"Yes," I grunted, trying to hold her still. "Stop standing there trying to look superior. A truly superior man would help without waiting to be asked."

"I will not," he snapped. "I am not a midwife – and certainly not for such a…creature." He spat the last word.

She began a loud wait of pain and protest, scratching and biting to get free of my hold.

The captain growled something violent sounding in her direction and she whimpered and tried to crawl to the furthest corner of the room.

"Hold still!" I implored, trying to bring her back. "If she keeps moving this way she is going to strangle the baby with his own umbilical cord." Perhaps if he understood how dangerous the situation was, he would help. He seemed to acknowledge it, but he did not move. "Now, will you quit trying to scare her to death and help me?"

He slid his gun into its holster. "I believe I said no," he answered coldly.

I stood up, furious. "Captain Contreras, I am asking you to rise above your ignorant prejudices and help me save one life, possibly two."

"It would be better if they did not survive," he answered sharply.

I flew at him, incensed. Catching him unaware, I scratched and slapped and clawed. When he realized what was happening, he caught my wrists and held me at arm's length, staring in disbelief. "You are crazed," he pronounced.

"You are a pig," I spat, shaking free of him.

"You go too far, Dinah McKee," he warned, taking a step closer.

"Go ahead," I said, "beat me up. Show the world how great and mighty you are, *Capitan*, because you can hurt a woman."

His hand, already raised to strike, froze. "You try me," he muttered and lowered his hand. "You try me."

The woman cried out again, a sharp staccato complaint that reminded me, in some perverse way, of the machine gunfire I'd been hearing all evening. "Captain, I'm not asking you to perform brain surgery on her. I'm not even asking you to get involved in the birthing process – I know that would be too much to ask of a man like you. I just want you to hold her still while I try to reposition the baby."

He caught my shoulder roughly as I started to kneel again. "What do you mean 'too much for a man like you'?" he demanded. "What is the meaning of that?"

I was struggling with the woman, but I risked a moment and a hand to brush my hair away where it stuck to my cheek and covered my eyes. I managed a superior smile at the same time. "It's a fact that men as macho and image conscious as you seldom have the stomach to witness the birth process."

He stood above me, almost speechless with rage. He lifted his hand again, to wipe away the accusation hanging in the air, but it trembled with feeling. He pointed toward the door, instead. "I have seen," he said with indignation, "men die in battle and have not shut my eyes to that. How do you dare suggest..." he stopped. "Do you dare suggest that I am a coward?"

I shrugged. "It's just a fact that men-"

"It is a lie."

It was a mistake to flinging down such a challenge in front of the captain was not necessarily going to encourage him to help me. I sighed. "All right, Captain." I eased the woman to her side and rubbed her back to ease some of the pain. "You men sure are eager to get the woman pregnant, but you don't want to have anything to do with her or the baby once that's accomplished," I muttered.

She wasn't comforted by my actions, moaning piteously for all the saints in Heaven to have mercy on her. I looked up at him. "Well?" I demanded angrily. "Are you going to help?"

To my surprise, he sighed and dropped to his knees. "Very well, what shall I do?"

A wave of relief washed over me. With his help, we might have a chance of saving one life, maybe two. "Get around there and hold her down by the shoulders. If you are willing to speak to her in any civilized manner, you might tell her not to push."

"To push?" he repeated, kneeling at the top of the mat, and wrestling the girl's heaving shoulders flat.

"Not so hard!" I warned. "Just hold her still, not tie her down."

His eyes flashed a dangerous fire that, on any less dramatic occasion, would have sent chills of fear down my spine. I looked into the girl's eyes and tried to smile, encouragingly. "Not so hard," I said, softly.

The girl's eyes were vacant, now and the wild cries had subsided into barely audible moans. The moment of triumph passed as I tried to work my way to the baby. There was a lot of blood already pooling between her legs.

"That face," he said. "It doesn't look good."

I didn't look up at him. "No, it doesn't."

He let go of the girl's shoulders. "Then we should go-"

"Hold her! Hold her! Can't you do anything right?" I cried as the girl suddenly began to squirm again.

He put his hands down on her shoulders, heavily. There would be bruises tomorrow, I thought. But, he didn't react to my insult. In fact, his voice, when he spoke, was soft, almost cajoling. "Dinah, as soon as we are missed, there will be a swarm of armed rebels coming this way in search of us. We do not have the luxury of staying to fight a lost battle."

"I know, I know." I rubbed sweat from my forehead with my sleeve. "Not much longer, now."

Chapter Three
The Camp

The captain leaned forward to look at her progress, and pulled back sharply. When he saw me smile to myself, he stiffened and leaned forward again. The expression on his face went from contempt to uncertainty to amazement. "Have you done this before?"

"Not under these circumstances," I said through clenched teeth. "But, I have delivered a child before." I flicked a curious glance at him, impressed at the way he resisted the need to look away that was written over his face. "Haven't you ever seen a child being born before?"

"It is something women keep to themselves in this country," he said. "Men do not intrude, and that's as it should be."

I was momentarily distracted from my task. "You mean you did not even stay to see your own children born?"

He rocked back on his haunches. "I have no children."

"I see." I looked at his hands, white knuckled against the woman's shoulders. There was no ring, but that did not signify anything in Latin countries.

"That I am aware of," he finished.

"I see," I repeated. "I would have thought…" I stopped as the girl began to buck and writhe again.

"No." He used his knees to hold her shoulders down as he pushed at clawing hands. "I am not married."

I sensed a danger, a new one, within myself. "Married to your career, no doubt," I said, with just a bit more sneer than was necessary or intended.

He did not seem to take offense. "It happened that way, *si*." He surprised me by smiling. "In that we are alike, no?"

The idea that I had anything in common with such a callous monster sent a shiver through me. "I suppose. No, no, she's pushing again. Make her stop."

He barked out an order and the girl cried in protest and fell silent. "Why should she not?" he asked me.

"If she pushes the baby before he is turned," I explained, "it will cause massive internal injuries for her, and will probably strangle the baby."

He started to say something to the girl, but I cut him off. "Don't tell her that, she is scared enough."

He sat back, glaring at me.

He didn't like being ordered around, that was clear. "Thank you," I said, in a conciliatory tone.

He nodded sharply and was quiet for a moment. "You do not wish children of your own?" he asked when the silence around us became too much for him.

The question caught me off guard. "Someday, I suppose," I answered almost breathlessly. The effort to turn the child was getting harder now, it almost required more strength than I had to give. Even so, I looked up at him. "You?"

"Circumstances have made it very unlikely," he answered, and I was disturbed to note that there was no apparent remorse in his tone.

"Because of the rebellion?" I asked, twisting the fetus one last time.

"Because of my life," he responded enigmatically.

There was a long silence. He stared off into a future or a history that I could not comprehend, and I didn't have time to try. Yet, even as I struggled to save the lives left in my hands, I couldn't help wondering about his. Had there been some long lost love in his past that prevented him from ever getting close to a woman again? I doubted very much if Captain Contreras ever got closer to a woman than a man does in bed. "There." I sat back on my heels and wiped more perspiration from my face.

He sat up. "Is it done?" he asked, glancing around, perplexed.

"Well, the baby has been turned," I explained. "Now we just have to wait for him to get here." She shot a glance at the mother, who was quiet, pale and still. "If he gets here."

He stood up, pulled his gun from his holster and examined it briefly. "*Vámanos*."

I released a shuddering breath. For one horrible moment I thought he was going to shoot the woman, or threaten her to give birth immediately, or some other horrifying or absurd response. "Not yet. Another fifteen minutes or twenty –"

"Now." He caught my arm roughly and jerked me to my feet. "We must go now. We have wasted too much time."

"Oh, but we can't!" I cried, twisting free. "She's too weak-"

"We cannot wait."

I stiffened, avoiding his outstretched hand. "I won't go with you."

"You will." He peered out the cloth door. "There is no argument about this."

I only needed to take one look at him and know that this time there would be no argument. For the first time since this ordeal started, I began to cry.

He looked at me in impatient surprise which turned to contempt. "Stop that," he commanded. "We are going now."

I rubbed at my tears, and held my ground. "You can't make me," I protested.

He muttered something ugly as he stepped over the girl on the floor and swept me up in one arm, tossing me over his shoulder as if I were a bag of grain. Ignoring my wriggling and kicking, he strode determinedly toward the path we had left hours before. At the log where we had parted company, he dropped me to my feet. "Now, we go."

I marched beside him, mutinously, every once in a while daring to cast a worried look over my shoulder. That poor woman is in so much pain, I thought, miserably. Only a man as arrogant and cold hearted as Captain Contreras would have dragged me out before I could ease that pain.

"Come faster," he commanded, picking up the pace of his march. "It is nearly dawn. We must get into camp before the first light."

"That baby would have come any time," I protested, sullenly. "It wouldn't have hurt to stay and help the woman through it."

"It could have killed us," he corrected sharply. Sensing my reaction to those words, he paused, with a sigh, and turned to face me. "Dinah, the child will die, no matter what you did or would do for it. This is a fact – an unpleasant one for you to accept – but, a fact all the same. She would not have nurtured the child. There was no maternal love there, no will for that child to live." He strode away.

I remained rooted to the spot, staring after him. "You are so certain that a 'rebel' isn't even capable of loving her child?" I sneered. "Captain, even animals have maternal instincts."

He stopped, lifted his eyes upward, as if seeking Divine support, and sighed. "You do not speak as much Spanish as I had thought, no?"

"Oh, what's that got to do with it?" I said, tiredly.

"Everything." He turned just enough that I could see his expression. It was one of disgust. "If you did, you would have heard what she said, how she prayed. Dinah, that child…" he paused, huffed a small sigh and returned to face me. "That child was fathered by one of my men. No," he insisted when I started to express my own disgust. "I am not proud of that admission. It is merely so. How could you love a child born of a night of rape and torture? You could not."

I cringed. I didn't have an answer. The question's implications seemed unthinkable.

He nodded solemnly. "Nor could she. If it were to survive birth, it would have starved to death in hours. It is more merciful, is it not, to never see sunlight than to die of neglect?" He didn't wait for my response, turning and marching away with greater speed than before.

"To never see sunlight," I repeated softly, and ran to catch up. "That sounds familiar."

"The psalmist David asked it of God for those who persecuted him," he answered, pushing aside a palm leaf. "Take care where you walk."

"How incongruous," I murmured, as I followed his careful step over the deadly, beautiful coils of the sleeping boa constrictor. I might have tightened my fingers around his, as I did.

He looked from the snake to me. "What does this mean, incon-incon…the word you just said?"

"Incongruous," I repeated, happy to put many steps between myself at that reptile. "It means unlikely in the circumstances or mismatched."

"That snake is hardly unlikely to the circumstances," he persisted. "So, what do you call incon…" he paused and tried again, "incongruous."

"Why, you, of course: a Communist soldier quoting the Bible."

He stopped and I cannoned into him this time. "I am not a Communist," he responded sharply. "I am only a soldier." A moment later, he added, "and I learned the Psalms at my mother's knee."

I nearly blurted out my surprise that he had a mother. "So, you are a Catholic?" I said instead.

"*Si,*" he answered curtly. "I was educated at a missionary school, in fact." A slow smiled crept over his face, transforming it yet again. "Where did you suppose I learned to speak English?"

"I did wonder."

"And you?"

I shook my head. "No, just a Christian."

"Many a sin has been committed under such a banner," he mused and moved on. "The camp isn't far from here." He stopped abruptly again and looked at me. "Have care how you speak," he warned. "Some of these men have some English, too. Do not be friendly or it will be misunderstood."

"From what I've seen of your men, they do not require a friendly gesture to misunderstand." When he glowered at me, I lowered my head and said, meekly, "Yes, Sir."

He smiled.

"How do I account for being with you?" I asked.

"I will answer for you," he decided. "If I give such orders, you should not be questioned. If you are, you pretend deafness, or that you speak no Spanish." He began to march.

"I don't think I can do that."

"You will not have to do it for long," he assured me. "Just let me assess the situation and then I will devise a plan to get you to the coast and the Marines." He stopped again, looking to the left and right, slowly, establishing landmarks. He put a hand out to keep me from moving. "Stay here and be very quiet. There will be sentries just ahead."

I clutched at his hand. "Are there any more snakes here?"

"Unlikely," he answered, "but stay very still, all the same. Keep your gun at the ready." He eased his hand from mine.

I let my hand fall to my waistband, not at all comforted by the hard handle there. "Very well."

"I will call you from the left, several paces off," he continued, pointing. "If you hear anyone approach who does not do this, shoot. We will sort it out later."

"*Vaya con Dios,*" I called impulsively.

His stride checked momentarily, then he marched away.

The stillness was dramatic and overwhelming. The night calls that had followed us through the jungle had ceased and there was an eerie silence in reverence of the last fleeting moments of darkness. I concentrated on the stillness, for it gave me a chance to monitor every movement of every leaf and creature near me. I schooled myself not to consider how alone and helpless I really was. In the night, back at the medical station, curled up on a cot and trying to sleep, I usually just listened to the movement of the animals outside our hut. Many times, on my way back from the lavatory, I had seen the golden eyes of a panther in the moonlight, death on four feet. Was that the same death watching me now as misty grayness overcame the darkness?

"Dinah?" I heard the voice to the left and the rustling to my right.

My hand tightened on the gun handle and I drew it out, slowly, as the two gleaming eyes appeared in the bush.

"Do not move, Dinah," the captain instructed in a low voice.

"You won't see me moving," I whispered, shakily, even as the gun trembled in my hands.

"Can you shoot?" he asked.

"No."

"Then, I beg you, do not breathe. I am directly behind you." The shot was like that of a cap pistol and I felt the flight of the bullet beside me. There was a roar and frantic steps and a rustle into the bush.

"Is it dead?" I whispered.

"No," he responded, stepping beside me, "I only aimed near enough to him to drive him away, which is fortunate. These cats are beautiful and are being hunted into extinction, but they are also deadly, and one must weigh the choices between dead animal and dead..." he stopped abruptly. "You were unexpectedly brave."

I wasn't formally introduced to anyone as we entered the encampment. For a headquarters step up overnight near what must be the front lines of the conflict, it was remarkably well ordered and efficient. There was even a hospital tent, already filling with wounded. Without asking permission, I went to work there, accessing and treating those wounds I was able, and making notes of those who would require greater skill than mine. This evidently supported an unspoken fiction that the captain had brought a nurse to aid in caring for the inevitable wounded.

While it chafed me that his action was being lauded as brilliant and heroic, I decided not to contradict the fiction. It seemed to grant me some immunity from the most egregious behavior. There were men who leered at me, or tried to touch me, but no one was aggressive beyond my ability to ignore them or thwart their efforts on my own. It amused me, however, that once he had met with his officers, he returned to the hospital, and stood near the door, watching me like some sort of diligent guardian.

While it seemed important to prove to these men that I was acting in a professional capacity, it was equally puzzling that I wanted to prove myself to a man who was the antithesis of everything I believed in. At what point did winning his respect begin to matter? I wasn't sure. I only knew that my need to prove myself had saved my life when I faced that panther in the clearing. If he had not been there, I know I would have brought that panther down on myself in my panic. In fact, I'd probably be dead now.

The wounds were more horrifying than anything I'd been exposed to so far. At the clinic we'd established in the village, I'd seen disease and malnutrition, and the results of accidents and cruelty, but I'd never seen injuries like these. I caught myself biting my lower lip until it bled, trying to keep my face expressionless, even while dressing the stumps of missing limbs, gaping wounds, exposed bones and organs. There were many times when I thought I might faint, but I would not allow myself the luxury of that weakness, knowing the captain's eyes were on me.

At midday, he intervened, forcing me away from the hospital, and, ignoring my protests and name-calling, took me to a large square tent of camouflage canvas. "Rest here," he instructed, cutting through another volley of complaints. He pushed me inside, where the air was still and heavy, but at least it offered shelter from a merciless sun and the smell of putrid flesh. "I'll send some food to you."

I felt my stomach roll, threatening. "Please don't," I begged, dragging the edge of my shirt across my brow. "Just some water, please. I don't think I could swallow anything else."

He reached for a canteen on a hook on the center pole of the tent. “Here. Have some brandy.”

It wasn’t until I’d unscrewed the cap, wiped the opening and raised the canteen to my lips that I realized that this was his canteen, the one we’d shared on our trek to the camp. Logic insisted this must be his tent. I lowered the canteen, eyeing him warily, but he wasn’t even looking at me.

“I’ll have some food sent to you.” He had turned his back and taken a couple of steps back to the tent flap. “You cannot continue to work without food. And,” he paused, and sent a glance over his shoulder that didn’t quite reach me, “I know you think you must continue.”

“Very well.” I took a sip and put the canteen back on the hook.

He was still standing at the tent door. “It has been a very long night for you,” he observed, with the same bemused study he had given me a lifetime ago, in the bedroom at his headquarters. “You must give yourself credit for all you have accomplished in it.” I didn’t look up or acknowledge his comment. “Trying to get out of the country with your skin intact, travelling through unfamiliar and dangerous territory, trying pointlessly to assist in that birth – and I would guess that caused the greatest emotional damage – the encounters with local…wildlife and several gruelling hours treating soldiers you despise.”

My innate response to refute such a suggestion caused me to look up, a protest in place, but not even habit could get me to deny how much I loathed those men and all they stood for. So, I merely shrugged and lowered my eyes.

"Yet, you have continued without a murmur of complaint." He looked me over, but there was nothing lascivious in the study. "Your dedication to duty would be remarkable, even in the best soldier."

I'm sure he meant it as a compliment, but it wasn't flattering to my point of view. "Shall I salute now, or wait until later?" I asked wearily, brushing away the curls that clung to my forehead. He was right about emotional damage. The image of such hopelessness in that mean little hut had already carved itself into my soul, leaving a scar that would probably last for life. The idea that I had surrendered to what he called 'inevitable' threatened to overwhelm me at any moment.

"Oh, no, only soldiers should salute. And you have other faults which would prevent you from being a worthy soldier."

"Yes, I know. I'm a woman," I snapped.

"Your greatest fault is your determination to say whatever comes to your mind, even at your peril," he answered, irritably.

I was actually proud of that statement, even though he had flung it at me like an insult. "It's one of the rights my country fought for," I answered, standing a little straighter with pride. "It's what this country is fighting for." That poor woman, giving birth alone...my heart twisted. No matter what he had maintained, I couldn't believe that the woman would willfully allow that child to die.

"Are you faint?" he asked abruptly, jumping forward to pull the canteen down again. "You have gone pale."

I brushed my brow again with my fingertips, feeling pressure in my head. "I'm tired, that's all, I murmured, turning away from the brandy. There, tucked under the cot, I saw my bag. I felt myself blush. "I do need to rest." I looked at the cot, prepared for no less than the commanding officer of the camp. "Do you think I could sleep for a little while?"

Captain Contreras bowed stiffly and gestured for me to lie down. He put the canteen back on the hook, and impulsively offered me his arm, as if he thought I might be too frail to lie down on the cot on my own. "Will you be all right?" Even his voice seemed to doubt my condition.

"I will be, if you leave me alone," I muttered.

"You aren't so frail that you can't keep from lashing out with that whip-like tongue," he scolded. Yet, a strange smile rested on his lips as I eased myself onto the cot, a smile that belied the harshness of his words. "I will send you some food," he repeated.

"No, no." Urgently, I caught his hand. "If you'd only let me rest."

"Very well, *Senorita*." He covered my hand with one of his. "Rest and I'll make the arrangements to take you over the border."

I shifted to make myself comfortable against the stiff cot. "Thank you," I said sleepily.

He backed toward the door. "I will see that you are not disturbed.

Of course, I had no intention of sleeping. As soon as I heard his shouted orders moving away from the tent, I got up and rummaged through my bag and found a bottle of antiseptic, which I tucked into one pocket, and I put the gun he had given me in the other. The tent was tied down at all four corners, so it was a simple thing to untie one flap and survey the area. Once I was satisfied that no one would see me, I slipped out, and scurried from tent to tent, Jeep to Jeep and tree to tree until I was out of the camp.

I knew that I had to be near the village, since the camp had been made in a natural clearing at the end of the footpath we had followed all night. If I followed the perimeter, just the way we had come, I could find the hut where I had left that unfortunate woman. I found a familiar sign post not too far away, and stepped out onto the road. It was empty, but I recognized a fence painted red, off in the distance, and I began to run. I suppose I shouldn't have been out in the open like that, no bringing attention to myself by running, but I didn't have much time, and I didn't want to waste what little I had stepping over sleeping snakes.

As I ran, I tried to keep my mind a blank, and not worry if I was running right into a battle, or across the sights of a sniper. I certainly didn't want to think about what the captain would do if he realized I had disobeyed his direct orders. I really didn't think about anything except the chance of saving that baby.

When I saw the house with an orange striped cloth in the doorway, I stopped running and began to walk slowly, looking from side to side, ready to jump at the first unnatural sound; there could rebels or soldiers in any of the huts. But it was quiet. The air was so still that not even dust stirred as I walked.

At last, I heard something, an almost unearthly wail. It was soft, but it was heart wrenching. I raced to the hut at the end of the road, and pushed the cloth aside. "Oh, no!" I moaned. I was too late.

I did my best to comfort the woman, to ease her physical pain. There was nothing I could do for her emotional pain, except wrap the infant in the cleanest cloth I could find, and try to give them both some dignity. I had a feeling the mother would be seeing her child again, very soon.

I don't know how I managed to hold back my tears until I stumbled out of the hut. Staggering across the road, I leaned against the stone water trough, and sobbed. I had failed. Now I had no alternative but to go back to the encampment and whatever fate awaited me there.

I must have lost track of time, somewhere, because dusk was falling as I found the footpath and turned in the direction I hoped was the camp. I really wasn't sure. I wasn't sure of anything at that moment. Why was I here? What good could I possibly do?

They surrounded me so fast, laying hold of me and dragging me away from the road, and the path so fast I didn't have time to reach for the gun before it was yanked from my pocket. I didn't even have time to scream.

There were probably a half a dozen of them, in their spoiled, smelly clothes. I didn't recognize any of them as the captain's men, but I did know the uniform. They dragged me toward a campfire, lit carelessly in the thick of the brush, where it felt as if I was being passed around like a good joke, their hands hurtful and probing. Even in my emotionally numbed state, I knew exactly what they had in mind. There would be no chance to plead my case, and I had seen the evidence of their savagery already.

I felt as if I had been in a continual state of panic since I'd first heard of the evacuation the day before, but each event heightened my fears, and lessened my ability to think coherently. The very fact that I could be pulled off a road in this manner, instead of remaining in the reasonable safety of the army camp was testament to my poor judgment, but now I was starting to understand terror, the heart stopping, blinding terror that closed up my throat so that I could not scream, where the sound of my elevated heart rate pounded in my ears, and where breathing was no longer a subconscious routine but required constant effort to sustain.

The laughter around me was ugly, the grip around my waist was like steel, and the hands that thrust their way under my shirt were rough, with broken nails that scratched my skin. The one who held me tried to kiss me, his mouth tasted of tobacco and some kind of alcohol, which sickened me as he tried to force my mouth open.

My head was starting to spin, my stomach starting to churn. I knew I was either going to faint or be violently ill, or possibly both, but it wouldn't stop these men. I wanted to pray, but I couldn't pull words together to say anything.

The rustle of some bushes nearby, drew their collective attention, and they all reached for guns, but the rapid fire Spanish came from a familiar voice, and the figure that stepped into the clearing was, if not friendly, as least a blessed relief. "Javier!"

His eyes fixed on me in surprise. Then they dropped, slowly, deliberately, to the hand exposing my breast. If I had been aware of anything more than my fear, I would have been embarrassed to be so exposed, and gratified to feel the frisson of guilt that ran through my captor's body.

The captain barked out an order in words so fast and so angry I didn't understand the words, but those around me certainly did, and the effect was so extraordinary, even I could see it. To a man, they paled, looked in my direction and then back to him. I was released, even pushed away, and I staggered toward the captain, who caught me and held me tightly at his side. "Oh, Captain," I sobbed.

"Be silent," he hissed, and barked orders again.

The man who had held me and groped me, trembled again, stammering out something that I thought meant "I didn't know." He said it repeatedly as the captain's men moved toward him. His protest grew louder and more shrill.

I buried my face in the captain's chest as the shots were fired. "Oh, Captain," I sobbed. And then I fainted.

I awoke on the cot where I had been put to bed earlier that day and, at first, I thought the entire episode must have been a nightmare. But, the captain was sitting on a wire crate, watching me, and his grim expression made it clear that I had not dreamed one horrible moment of it. The memory made me ill and I leaned over the edge of the cot and vomited.

He rushed forward with the canteen of brandy, which had been at his side, indicating that he had been drinking while I had been recovering from my faint. He tried to lift my head and hold the metal container to my lips, but I shook my head and tried, feebly, to push him away. "Leave me," I implored.

He waited until I was finished and had rolled back onto the cot. "Why did you disobey me?" he demanded.

"I had to go," I explained raggedly. "I had to try and help."

"And did you?" he asked as if he already knew the answer.

I wondered if he even cared. "No."

"So, in order to witness the end of a hopeless life, you risked being mistaken for a rebel sympathizer, risked whatever is left of your virtue, and possibly risked your life."

"I had to try." Was it possible that his face was just a little pale beneath his deep tan? "I told you, a life is a life to me. I don't care about your silly politics. I j-just wanted to save a b-baby." Knowing that the tears were coming no matter how I tried to stop them, I sat up and tried to roll to the end of the cot.

He pushed me back into the bedding roughly. "Stay. You will sleep here tonight."

"But, you said you would take me-"

"You will stay here tonight and every night until I can take you across the border."

"The border? You mean the coast. You said you would take me to the Marines."

He pushed thick, black hair back from his brow with the back of his hand. "Your Marines have pulled back too far from shore for us to communicate with them, so I am taking you across the border to the American Embassy in Guatemala. Coast or border, it matters not. You are committed to me until the end of this ordeal."

"'Committed'?" I repeated. "That's an odd word to use." I turned my face back to the canvas wall. "Why?"

"Dinah McKee."

Something in his tone compelled me to look back at him.

He was frowning. Of course, he was always frowning, but there was something unnerving about this frown. It was also perplexed. "Do you understand how I managed to take you away from those men tonight?" He flipped his hand, a gesture I was beginning to realize was his way of saying 'look at both sides.' "Do you suppose it was a simple thing to march in and order them to free just *any* woman when they had not had one in so very long?"

Something tight pulled around his eyes, and drew his mouth into a grim line. "Do you?"

"No," I conceded quietly. A horrible idea occurred to me and I gasped. Surely he had not implied that I was *his* woman – not again?

He straightened his shoulders, lifting his chin a little. "I told them the only thing they would respect in those circumstances. I told them you were my wife."

I gasped again, this time in surprise. "What?"

His voice roughened. "Now I am bound to a pound of trouble with hair as white as a flag of surrender. I am trusting that you will be worth it." His gaze dropped over me lewdly.

"You can't mean…" my voice trailed off. I'd always thought I was a modern woman, on the battle lines of equality, and here I was on the verge of a maidenly faint because some man was staring at my breasts. I made myself stand up straight, and meet his eyes. "Everyone must know you aren't married to me, and if you tried to…if you…" I found myself more maidenly than I had expected. I couldn't form the words.

"What will they think?" I think my sudden discomposure amused him. "They will think their *Capitan* must make love to his wife, no? It will give them something to think about besides battle."

"Oh!" I turned away, recalling the scene with revulsion. "But, that…that man…"

"I had him shot," he admitted with a shrug.

"I know." I covered my eyes and fell back into the cot, again roughly. I could recall it so vividly it was as if it were happening again the tent. "Did you have to kill him? He never...he never did that."

When he didn't respond, I lifted one hand tentatively and looked in his direction. The pride had faded from his expression and something similar to fear replaced it. "He would have, Dinah. Do not think otherwise. It was their intent that they all rape you before they killed you," he finished deliberately.

I shuddered, and my stomach churned, threateningly. "But, when you said that I was your – what you said I was-"

"I had him shot because that is exactly what they would expect me to do if I found another man with his hands on my wife," he explained angrily. "*Por Dios,* Dinah McKee, I did it to save your *life*. They would have had no fear or remorse if they killed you. A woman is only a woman and meant to be shared by anyone who can catch her, unless she is bound before God to another man. They would not have believed you were my wife unless I killed him for putting his hands on you."

I couldn't stop shivering. He had ordered the death of a man simply to keep me from being raped and possibly killed. And now he expected me to repay him with the very thing he killed that man for wanting. The hypocrisy made me sick. That I was, on some level actually grateful to the man made me even more so. "Very well, Captain," I said, quietly. At least, under these circumstances, I was safer than trying to get to the border alone. I suppose my virginity was a very small price to pay.

"Even in our country a woman would not call her husband by his rank, but by his name. You know my name – you used it quick enough tonight. Please continue to use it."

I sat up, rubbing my arms, where my skin had prickled with goose bumps. "Very, well, Javier." I looked toward him, waiting for him to pounce.

He was looking down his nose at me, making a face.

I looked down, too. My clothes were torn and muddy, there were bruises on my arms and legs; there was a purplish handprint on one breast and I knew I had at least one bruise on my cheek, My hair was tangled and dirty. Not exactly an appetizing prospect, even to him. "Could I at least wash my face and comb my hair first?"

He glanced toward the door, and when he looked back at me, he was smiling. Not leering, not laughing, not mocking, but smiling. "You have no fears for tonight, *Senora* Contreras," he said the name with humor. "Soon, but not tonight." He looked around the tent. "I will arrange for food and a bath, and some clean clothes – with buttons," he added, reaching out to tug my torn shirt together. "Your..." he extended one finger and caught the broken strap of my bra. "You can do something about this? I would not recommend that you walk around without it. I would hate to shoot another man."

He stood straight again, turned on his heel and marched out of the tent, leaving me alone.

And yet, I wasn't alone; faces flashed before me again. Faces in pain, hateful faces, proud faces, evil faces, dying faces. I wasn't given long to catalog them or plead for forgiveness. There was a tap at the wooden frame of the tent. I pulled the shreds of my shirt together tightly and called, "Yes."

It was one of the young men I had seen in the hospital area. There was a new respect in his eyes as he entered, a basin of water in his hands, a large khaki shirt draped over his arm. *"Para usted, senora,"* he told her, pantomiming a vigorous face scrubbing after he put the basin on the wooden crate where Captain - that is, where Javier had been sitting.

"Thank you," I told him, disliking the curious gleam that suddenly sparkled in his eyes as he looked around the tent. It was clear he was astounded that his captain lived so simply and equally astounded that his captain would marry an American woman. There was an invasion of Javier's privacy in that gleam and I met it with obvious resentment.

He dropped his eyes and dug into his pocket, producing a small bottle of what appeared to be hydrogen peroxide from the infirmary stores.

"Thank you again," I said, letting the censure creep into my voice.

He nodded and backed out.

Once he was gone, I gingerly removed what was left of my shirt and bra. It felt good to scrub myself with warm water, and to treat my cuts. As I rummaged in the bag for my hairbrush and my sewing kit, the tent flap was torn aside and Javier appeared.

Instinctively, I covered my breasts with my hands. "What are you doing here?" I looked over his shoulder at the tent flap. I was certain I had tied it securely.

I could have predicted that his eyes would go to and fix on my hands, and they did. But, after a moment, he surprised me by actually looking up to my face. "I came to inquire after my... wife." He bowed slightly. "I see you will survive."

"Get out of here," I hissed, frantically. "I'm not dressed."

He offered me the shirt, making no effort to keep his eyes off me. "Dress yourself, *mi esposa*," he said, dryly. "And surely there is no need for such modesty between man and wife."

I made a sound of exasperation and turned my back on him and slid into my bra, hoping that I tied this strap more securely than those of the tent door. I was startled when his fingers gathered up the fabric and fastened it. "Really, *Senor*, I didn't expect you to be so adept at closing the clasp of such an item," I said, in a shaky voice.

"I am, perhaps, more adept at the opening," he chuckled.

"*That* I believe." I slid into the shirt he had provided.

"You will be relieved to learn that word has been spread that the penalty for any disrespect to you is death," he announced proudly.

"Terrific, I'm a walking death sentence," I muttered, finding myself hopelessly tangled in the sleeves.

"You will be treated with dignity and respect," he assured me as he began rolling up one of the sleeves. "As befitting any possession of mine."

I jerked away from him. "Let's get this straight, buster," I snapped. "I may be beholden to you for my life, and I'll submit to your...your rape," I stumbled over the word, "but you will never, ever own me."

Javier's hands hovered in mid-air. His haughty attitude crumbled into anger, and his fists clenched, but the violence I expected never materialized. His eyes slid over me again. "*Senora*," he cajoled, pulling me back toward him, "when God unites a man and woman, he gives that woman to that man. He is responsible for her, as is his horse or his weapon, or his land. Is that not possession?"

"Your *horse*?" I repeated, disgusted. When he started to explain, I held up a hand. "Even if that were not the most offensive argument I've ever heard for marriage, we are not united by anyone but your big mouth." His fist clenched again, but I pretended not to see the threat. "What you're going to do to me is fornication in the eyes of your Church. And it's rape in the eyes of the law." For a moment, I entertained the wild hope that such an argument might deter him.

For a moment, he seemed to be giving weight to my words, but then he shrugged and began rolling up my other sleeve. "Then I pray to see a priest before I die," he answered evenly. A wicked little smile slid across his face. "For I shall surely need confession."

I backed just out of his reach and crossed my arms over my chest, staring at him hard. "Then you do intend to rape me."

He shook his head. "That is your choice, *Senora*, not mine. I only know that I intend to bed you." He waited for me to react to his statement. I did not and he sighed, resignedly. "If you want it to be rape, then I shall comply."

Chapter Four
The Concession

Our eyes locked. We might have been equally matched in determination and wit, but he had a gun and brute strength. If I couldn't out argue him, this wasn't going to end well for me.

There was a movement at the tent flap and a dark faced, older man appeared. "*Capitan*, I-" He broke off as he realized that he had interrupted a very intimate moment.

Javier jerked around, his angry expression melting at the sight of the intruder. "Roberto, you must never come into my tent uninvited," he warned gently. "My wife might be dressing or in some other delicate situation."

"Your wife?" The sunken eyes were wide with confusion. Suddenly, he straightened up and executed a perfect bow. "A thousand apologies, *Senora*," he said in heavily accented English. "I did not know you were in the camp." His eyes darted toward Javier for a moment, and there was disapproval there.

It seemed to have some sort of chastising effect. "She's American. I need to get her safely out of the country," he explained tersely. "It wasn't safe to leave her behind. And she is a nurse, so, naturally, she insisted on coming here first to see if she could help in any way."

I dropped down onto the edge of the cot in amazement. He was a much better actor than I would have ever suspected. But, was Roberto a good actor, too? Or was there actually a *Senora Capitan* somewhere and Javier had lied to me.

Roberto nodded another bow in my direction. "If I can be of any use to you, *Senora*."

I wondered if I had found an ally in this old man. I worked up a smile for him. "*Gracias*, Roberto. It's comforting to know that I may rely on someone here."

Roberto flicked another look at Javier. "It is my pleasure."

The captain watched the exchange with a furrowed brow. "Robert, I will put my wife's safety in your hands whenever I am not nearby," he announced. "Dinah has already had one frightening experience here."

Two, if you count meeting you, I thought darkly.

"*Si, Capitan*," Roberto promised.

We remained there, looking from one to another in a strange silence and I had the feeling that Roberto knew that Javier wasn't really married, and if I knew that, then surely Javier knew. It would have been funny if it had not been so frightening.

Javier made an impatient sound. "Did you need something, Roberto?"

"*Si*, there is a question regarding Aluendez, to the north. If you could come and look at the new map?" Roberto said this, still looking at me.

Javier nodded sharply and then surprised us all by dropping a kiss to my cheek. "Sleep, Dinah, you will feel better in the morning."

I eased back on the cot as the two men left the tent, wondering if I would ever feel better again.

I woke to the rat-tat-tat of machine gun fire not far off. The sun was shining, but there were no morning birds, just the sound of the war and an Easterly wind. I had no trouble orienting myself to my surroundings for the events of the last twenty four hours swam in my thoughts all night. I raised my head slowly, stiff from my awkward position, and looked around the tent. The deep, even breathing I heard was at my side, where Javier had stretched out on the canvas floor beside the cot.

In sleep, he looked less forbidding, his jet hair falling into his dark face, the stern lines smoothed out of his expression, the grim determination around his mouth eased away. He sighed and stirred and I pulled back sharply, so that he wouldn't wake and find me leaning over him. He shifted again and frowned in his sleep. I had an irrational urge to reach out and comfort him, but it passed. The truth was, I was the one who needed comforting.

As if to verify my painful admission, the machine gun fire rattled again, like a snake in tall grass. I ducked, involuntarily, at the sound.

Javier turned and opened his eyes. They darted around the tent as if he was confused, and then they landed on me, and the confusion shifted to disbelief and then recognition. "Dinah," he said, sighing.

I watched him stretch, his broad chest bare and exposing tight coils of muscle. I'd encountered those muscles before, but it was still disconcerting to see them unabashedly bare. Under other circumstances, I think I would have found his body very attracted.

He looked toward me again, returning my study with a frank stare of his own, even going so far as to brush my hair away from my cheek where, I suspect, a very large bruise had developed. "You took a beating," he said, as if the pain were his own, and his touch was surprisingly tender. "Do you hurt much?"

I shook my head. It was true that I felt stiff and my movements were somewhat restricted by pain, but I wouldn't admit that to him. "I'll live."

"Undoubtedly," he said, dryly, and pulled himself into a sitting position so that we were eye to eye. "*Buenos días, mujer. ¿Cómo estás?*"

"*Muy bien,*" I answered, without thinking. After all, that was the conventional reply.

"You lie, *mi jita,*" he returned with a smile that seemed jarringly out of place. "You are not 'very good.' I have heard your Spanish. I know you know how to answer truthfully."

I nodded, again an expected reply. His appellation was a common endearment, usually reserved for children and I found that disturbing. I did want this man to think of me as nothing more than a helpless child, completely dependent on him. "My Spanish isn't good enough. How do I tell you that I'd rather be home in New Orleans, in my own bed, never having heard of this place, this war, or you?"

His sympathetic smile shifted into a full grin. "I think you have just done so." He patted my shoulder. "I will have you there as soon as I can." His gaze fell on the shirt that was far too big and consequently too revealing, and the grin evaporated. "Yes, as soon as I can."

At the sound of more gunfire, he pulled back as though he were breaking an embrace. "But, for now, I need to focus on this place, and this war. Listen." He cocked his head toward the door as another exchange of gunfire sounded. "It is very close."

"I know. I've been listening to it since just before dawn."

"That long?" He reached for the shirt he had rolled into a pillow, stood and shook it out, sharply. "I must go and investigate." He tugged the shirt on and pushed the tent flap aside. "Stay here." He left me.

I watched him go, and listened for his footsteps as long as I could distinguish them. It wasn't that I feared that he would return. It was that I feared he wouldn't. There had been a momentary intimacy that made me feel protected, an intimacy I'd never experienced with anyone before. For just a moment I wondered if I could fall in love with a man like him, or in a place like this. I decided I could not, but decided to keep my feelings under good control, just in case.

"As if I could," I said aloud, a moment later, pulling my hair brush from the bag. "He's a man who could only make love to his gun."

Almost in reply, there was another rattle of machine guns nearby. Hairbrush in hand, as if it was a weapon, I inched toward the tent flap and peered out. I could see nothing. What would happen to me if the battle overran the camp? I wondered. What would happen to me if Javier...I stopped. I wouldn't allow myself to even think such words. It wasn't that I am particularly superstitious, but in those circumstances, there was no point in asking for trouble.

As shadow grew on the ground in front of the tent and I backed away, stumbling onto the cot. I heard a little scratching sound on the canvas door. *"Si?"*

Roberto entered, with a steaming tin cup. *"Café, Senora,"* he said, his eyes discreetly averted.

"Gracias," I said, pointing to the folding table next to the bed with my hairbrush. Things couldn't be too bad if they were making coffee.

Roberto backed away, muttering something dour. I understood that he resented my intrusion in Javier's business. Believe me, Roberto, I thought, reaching for the cup, you don't resent it one tenth as much as I do.

"Perdóname, Senora." He was hovering at the tent flap, his head still slightly bowed.

"Forgive you? For what? I mean...*que*?" I knew I sounded impatient, but I was still fixated on the questions which had begun to swirl in my mind. How could the fighting have gotten so close to the camp, if the army was supposed to be driving the rebels back into the hills?

Roberto took my response to be permission and moved closer to the bed. "I must say..." he was searching for English words, "what is on my..." he pressed a fist to his chest.

"Heart?" I suggested.

He nodded. "Heart."

I wanted. Roberto waited, apparently holding his tongue until he had my permission to continue. I gestured impatiently. "Go on."

"It is a sin, *Senora*," he said. He didn't seem to have any difficulty finding those words.

"A...sin?" He knew the truth! Would he tell the others?

"It is a sin a man would bring his..." he pointed to the bed.

"Wife?" I hoped that was the word he wanted.

"Wife." He finally met my eyes, and there seemed to be no further struggle for the English language. "His most cherished possession, into a hell like this."

I tried not to let my relief show. He didn't know the truth – he didn't even suspect it. Javier was such a good commander that even his closest aide would not recognize his lie. "It couldn't be helped," I soothed. The man was obviously distressed that someone he admired might behave so thoughtlessly. "The war..."

"*Revolución*," he corrected me.

I wondered if Javier thought it was a revolution, but I didn't ask. "Revolution."

Roberto made a spitting noise that caused me to recoil. *"Es sólo una excusa para violar, saquear y asesinar a personas inocentes."*

I recognized just enough of his words too shocked by his accusations (even if I agreed with his assessment.) "Roberto," I warned in a hushed voice, "you mustn't talk that way. What if the captain were to hear-"

"He has already heard it, *mujer*." Javier had pushed the tent flap aside, and entered. "He has heard it a hundred times by now." He lowered the flap deliberately. "Roberto is a sentimental old fool who would be dead many times over he followed his heart instead of my head, and he knows it. He has that much in common with you. Is that coffee, Dinah?" He picked up the cup, lifted it to his lips and paused. "Does it gall you to share a cup with your husband?"

I looked toward the tent flap. Roberto had hustled away. "You are not my husband," I whispered, coldly. "And anyway, I was not aware my opinion counted here."

"You would prefer to become the woman of the camp?" he offered, wiping his mouth with his sleeve as he held the cup out to me.

I shook my head.

"Then be grateful that I lend you my name, Senora de Contreras, lest you find yourself tonight with a less congenial host."

That I wanted to stay with him even without the threat shamed me, and I lowered my head.

"What is this?" he demanded, fingering my chin and forcing it up. "Meek submission from my rebellious, rebel loving wife?"

"No!" I jerked away from his touch. "Leave me alone. Haven't I been through enough?"

"Have you?" he asked, his eyes once again drawn to the way his shirt fit over my chest. "I think not." His voice dropped even as he fell to his knees before me, shrugging out of his shirt. "Not nearly enough." His hands tightened around my shoulders and pulled me forward against him. His mouth forced mine open, his tongue exploring it.

I did not fight him; I knew he found my seduction as his due, and I tried to acquiesce despite the trembling throughout my body as his hands moved over me, lingering on my breasts. He handled them hungrily, molding them, caressing them, light a fire in them.

His tongue thrust deeper into my mouth as his hands separated the buttons of the shirt. He leaned forward, pressing his bare torso against mine. "Put your arms around me," he commanded hoarsely, as his mouth slid down my throat. "Touch me as I touch you."

I didn't want to. I wanted to resist. Protest. But, my fingers followed a path across his shoulders and down his back. His skin was hot and smooth and hard. As he forced me backward on the cot, his mouth fixing on my nipple, I began to think that this penalty might not be so horrible, after all…

Wait! I stiffened, my hands working to his chest to push him away. This man is a cruel, hate-filled captain of a vicious military regime, I reminded myself, who takes whatever he wants and this morning, he wants me. I tore my mouth from his.

He drew back with a frown. His hands moved sharply from my breasts to my upper arms, pinning me to the cot. "Dinah, you are not going to fight." It was a statement, not a question.

"I…I…can't." I twisted against his hold. "Please, Captain, I-"

He hissed at me. "You must not call me Captain. You must call me Javier, as a wife calls her husband by his name. And even if you are not my wife," he paused, and ran his tongue over my nipple, "I will most certainly treat you as such." For a moment his teeth tightened over the place where his tongue had just been, making me gasp. "With or without your consent," he added.

"Javier, please," I implored.

"You cannot lie to me, *mujer*," he mocked. "Your body says you want this as much as I do."

I continued to struggle. "No, please, there's something you-"

"*Capitan, per favor.*"

Javier froze over me. "*Sí?*" As the tent flap waited a baby-faced soldier. Javier gestured angrily to the boy as he moved his body just enough to shield mine from view.

The boy began to babble apologies, clearly even more embarrassed that I was by the scene. In all honesty, I was too relieved to be embarrassed.

I tugged my shirt closed and sat up, promising myself that I would never let Javier catch me alone in the tent again.

He turned back to me, saw that I was dressed, and forced a small smile around his frown. "Forgive me, *mi jita,*" he said with what might have been genuine regret. "Duty calls. I will return as soon as I can to finish...this." It wasn't meant as a promise. It was definitely a threat.

As soon as he was gone, I dived to the flap of the tent and tied it as securely as I could. I dug out my sewing kit and quickly repaired my bra strap. He wasn't going to find me so exposed again. I felt infinitely safer once that task was complete and I was safely back in that borrowed shirt. I tied it at the waist so it would fit more securely, not falling open at the collar to be so revealing. I brushed my hair and pulled it up in a no-nonsense chignon. I had no make-up or perfume with me so I was easily the least feminine creature these men would ever see. Feeling certain that I had obliterated any allure I might possess, I let myself out of the tent and walked around, carefully staying on the roads of packed dirt, but away from groups of soldiers or the perimeter where snipers might be hiding.

This was the first time I'd really looked around. The camp was situated on the edge of a wide, green expanse that was probably a tobacco field. Beyond that were purple mountains trimmed with tall evergreens. It was an impressive sight; the air was so clear and still I could pick out the details of rock and foliage on the mountainside easily five miles away. There were no sights like that in Louisiana, that was certain. It was hard to believe that I was sitting on the edge of a battlefield.

"It is beautiful, no?" Javier appeared unexpectedly and fell into step beside me.

"Yes," I agreed. My heart was hammering in fear and surprise. "I guess I'm not used to so much open area...or such mountains." I gestured toward the horizon. "It's really magnificent."

"You prefer the mountains of steel and glass, no doubt." He shook his head disdainfully. "And this you call freedom?"

"Well, and the freedom to come to places like this if I wanted to," I answered hotly.

"Your concept of freedom confuses me, Dinah," he sighed.

"That's because you consider freedom your particular purview and no one else's," I said pointedly. "My greatest freedom is the freedom to choose, Captain."

"Ah." He nodded and his black eyes swiveled from the tobacco field back to me. "And you choose a gang rape over the lovemaking of one man?"

"What do you mean?"

His hand snaked out to catch the front of my shirt and dragged me against him. "You forget my name one more time and I will denounce you and deliver you to them personally." He released me and I staggered away from him.

"I'll…I'll try to remember," I stammered, smoothing the shirt into place with nerveless fingers.

"It is not a hard name to remember. Here, I wrote it down for you." He offered me a scrap of brown paper that smelled like coffee.

I glanced down at it. Javier Enrique Diaz y Contreras. "I didn't realize it was spelled with a J." I shook my head, feeling foolish. "I should have realized it, but I never even thought…" I shoved the paper into my pocket. "Thank you for writing it out."

He nodded and looked out to the fields she had been admiring. It was difficult to conceive of such a scene being deadly, yet it was as poisonous as the prettiest viper sleeping in the sun. "Well," he said, weighing his words. "As you have guessed, the battle is pulling back in this direction. That is good and that is bad."

"How can it be good?" I asked. I could think of nothing uplifting about sitting on the edge of a battlefield.

"Because, it means our men in the north are driving the insurrections south to us," he answered. "We will attack from the flank and the rebels will be surrounded and destroyed."

I winced at the description and his obvious satisfaction in the plan. "I'd hate to see your idea of bad," I muttered.

"Ah, Dinah, the battle will cut off our lines to the border," he answered.

I turned sharply. "You mean…?"

"You will be with me much longer than either of us anticipated."

"Much longer?" I repeated. "How long is much longer?"

He shrugged. "Who knows? It depends on how long it takes to wipe out these…" he snapped his fingers toward the tobacco fields. "A week? Perhaps two. You will stay here in the camp, of course, until it is safe to take you the border. I will not expose you to the battlefield."

"You mean, you're going to leave me behind?" I couldn't believe it. Perhaps this was his idea of punishment for my resistance earlier. How petty. How like a man.

He stared at me with equal disbelief. "That is precisely what I mean. You do not think a battlefield is the place for a woman – surely that is not possible, even for you."

"You've brought me this far," I shot back.

His mouth tightened grimly. "There is a difference between this camp, where there are armed guards, medical care, regular meals and the privacy of tents and the place where we are going, Dinah McKee. Do not fool yourself to think otherwise."

"What if there are wounded?" I countered. I didn't want to stay behind. "You'll need a nurse."

He smiled without humor. "Of course there will be wounded; it happens at such times. I shall not let you near them."

"Oh, you won't."

He heard the defiance in my voice and his eyes narrowed. "No, I will not." There was a note of finality in his voice.

"But, it's m-"

Javier put a hand to my mouth. "Your first duty is to me. How would it look to my men to have my wife caring for the wounds of the enemy?"

"The same as it would if they saw me treat the wounds of your own men," I snapped, shaking free of him. "As hard as it might be for you to believe, some of your men might need medical attention in the field, too. Just look at what we found yesterday when we arrived."

He backed up a step, stunned. "You would risk your life to treat these men, as well, despite your experiences?"

"Look, Javier," I said with ragged patience, "all politics aside, a life is a life to me. Whether it was one of those so-called rebels for whom you have nothing but contempt, or one of your own soldiers. Why, I'd even risk my life to save your insufferable hide."

He snatched at my arm, angrily. "You will have care how you speak to me," he warned.

"Let go of me, Javier," I demanded, as calmly as I could, forcing my eyes up to the fiery rage in his. I would not submit now. It was too important that he recognize me as a force in my own right, not a child to pat on the head and push aside.

His eyes widened suddenly. "You do not command me, *mi jita*," he reminded me, his grasp on my arm twisting slightly.

I steeled myself against showing pain. "And you do not command *me*," I repeated firmly. "Let me go. I'm not yours to command or abuse. Now, let go of my arm." I waited a breath. "Please."

He released me, more in surprise than obedience. I had the impression no woman had ever stood up to him before; he wasn't expecting a five foot even blond American girl to stare him down. Frankly, I didn't think I'd get away with it. "Very well." He backed away, brushing at the front of his shirt as if I had somehow soiled him. "But not because you command me. Because it is more convenient for me to do so."

I started to smile. "I thought it was because I said please."

His eyes narrowed and his voice got cold and deadly. "Remember: You do not command me, Dinah McKee."

I stopped smiling. "And you do not own me, Javier Enrique Diaz y Contreras." I turned sharply and marched away.

"Perhaps not." His voice followed me, softly. "But, I will possess you."

I lifted my head, but did not look back as I walked away.

As dusk fell, and I huddled near a fire as the air had gotten cold without warning, a messenger, bloody and torn, stumbled into the camp. Without thinking, I rose at the sight of his wounds, and rushed toward him. I was astonished and angry when Javier intercepted me, holding me back. "But, Javier," I protested, still trying to get to the poor man, "he's hurt."

Javier hollered out something and suddenly I was caught at the waist by another soldier, lifted off my feet and held back. "Take her to my tent," Javier barked and I was dragged away like a poorly trained dog.

I was flung on the bed savagely, as if the sweaty, beardless young man enjoyed having me at his mercy. I hadn't even noticed him nearby, all my attention had been focused on Javier, but as I pulled myself upright on the cot, I was very aware of his hungry eyes, looking and lingering on parts of me no man had the right to see. I felt as if he were stripping me bare with that black stare. Oh, no, I thought, closing my eyes against that ugliness, I guess Javier has made good on his threat. But…why would he allow it to happen in his tent?

When I opened my eyes, the young man was groping himself, as if to display his prowess or superiority. The gesture sickened me. Please, I prayed, not this one. I wanted to crawl back into a corner and out of his reach.

"Senora likes men, no?" he asked, licking his lips as they pulled back into an ugly gash across his face. I'd once heard someone describe an expression as 'a wolfish smile' but I had never been able to imagine what it looked like. Here it was in the flesh.

I sat up straight, expressing my contempt with a curl of my own lips. "Get out of here." I pointed toward the tent flap, imperiously, adopting the same air I had used successfully on Javier.

"I like women," he went on, moving a little closer to the cot. "I have not had a woman in a long time."

"Well, you're not going to be with me, Buster," I snapped, watching his hands as they hovered near the button fly of his uniform. "I happen to be m-married to your commanding officer."

The young man shrugged. "Who will be dead in a day, maybe two, and then you will belong to us."

"How dare you?" I said, imitating Javier's low, lethal voice. "How dare you speak to me like that, or say things about your captain?" I had assumed that sharing Javier's name made me sacrosanct among his men; he had said as much himself. I hadn't counted on being part of his bequest to his faithful followers. I hadn't counted on him dying. "And he is not dead now, though you might be if you don't get out of this tent, this minute."

His grin only became more insolent. "It is interesting, no? Here you are, his…" he paused, frowned and then grinned again, "his wife. I came up this morning from headquarters in town. In the town, two days ago, it is said there was a woman captured among the rebels. They say she had hair as white as clouds –"one grimy hand flicked out to brush the hair from my cheek -"and eyes bluer than the sky."

I slapped his hand away, repulsed.

"And it is also said that the *Capitan* was there, saw her, and took her to warm his bed before the battle. They say she disappeared after the *Capitan* left..."

I swallowed, hard. So someone knew the truth; soon, everyone would know it. Javier's reputation would be destroyed and he would be labeled a liar. Why should I care about Javier's reputation? "Are you trying to make me jealous with your silly stories?" I demanded, haughtily.

"What is this...jealous," he struggled with the unfamiliar sound. "I only want one thing from you." He lunged, like a jungle cat, forcing me backward onto the cot.

I didn't even have a chance to scream. His mouth was on mine savagely, his hands pawing at my shirt. Strangely, as his smell choked me, and his hands bruised me, all I could think about was that Javier was right: his lovemaking would be infinitely better than this. But where was he?

"Mendez!" The name was like a whip across my attacker's back. He jerked back, stiffened and slid down to the floor. In two steps, Javier was upon him, dragging him off Dinah with the blackest rage mirrored in his face. One powerful fish sent the man to his knees again and another, delivered the force and efficiency of a pile driver, sent him, unconscious, to the floor.

Without even a glance toward where I knelt, white knuckled at the end of the cot, he pushed the flap open and eyed the camp. "The curse of having a beautiful woman in a camp full of hungry men," he said, "is that there will always be those who would risk their life for the taste of her kisses. Alvarez, Amando, *vamanos*."

Two burly men appeared at the tent flap, took in the situation, understood and moved wordlessly to remove the unconscious marauder.

"You...you aren't going to shoot him, are you?" I asked. I loathed and despised the man for what he did, but I didn't want him to die for it.

Javier shook his head, still refusing to look at me. "He will only wish I had." His shoulders rose and fell in a deep sigh. "He only took what every man here would try to take if he thought he had the chance. He thought I would be so busy with the informant that I would not catch him. He did not count on the man's wounds being so severe that he would die within minutes of his arrival."

I gasped in protest of yet more waste.

Javier dropped the tent flap into place and turned to look at me at last. "That is why I would not allow you to treat him, Dinah," he explained. His words were terse but there was a softness, a kindness in them. "He was so badly wounded that even I could not look at him. I knew that he would soon die, not matter what you did. Why force you to carry those memories in here?" He touched his forehead.

"I should have..." No, he was right. I shook my head.

He took a step nearer, looking at me for the first time. "Are you hurt?"

I shook my head again. "Not even so frightened," I admitted, rearranging my shirt. "It seems to have happened so much lately. I think I'm just...mad."

For a moment, he chuckled, but sobered at once. "I am glad you are not hurt."

I reached out to touch him and drew back, realizing that he was struggling with his own pain. "I'm sorry the boy died, Javier."

He did not look at me again. He drew breath deep into his chest and let it out slowly. "He died bravely." He lifted his head. "One can always admire that."

It was clear he didn't want to discuss it ever again. I looked around the tent looking for another subject to sweep away those painful thoughts. "Do you really think I'm beautiful?"

He turned toward me, sharply, in disbelief. There was a denial on his tongue. His shoulders sagged in defeat. "Yes."

I smiled. "Thank you."

"Too beautiful, in fact," he ground out. "You are distracting not only to me, but to my men. It is because..." he raised a hand in a grasping gesture, as if reaching for the right analog. "You are like a snowflake on a sun parched desert. We have not even seen snow before. So we spend all our time trying to catch it, and it is really..." he opened his hand, "nothing."

All the pleasure I had derived in being considered beautiful was destroyed by his attitude. His remarkable compliment was laden with accusation, making me feel guilty for being blond and fair skinned. "I'm sorry, *Senor,*" I said, flatly. "It was never my intention to become involved with you and your men. But, surely, you, of all people, understand how it is when one has a duty to perform. It must be performed – no matter the cost." I unfolded my legs and stood. "And I realize that I, too, have a cost to pay."

He didn't even look at me. He merely shook his head. "Not tonight. You have been through enough." He scratched his heavy beard thoughtfully. "Perhaps tomorrow, if you can avoid being attacked for one entire day..."

"I did not ask for that to happen." I pointed out.

"You ask for it by your very presence," he argued. "Your walk, your bearing, the tilt of your head – they entice a man to lose control."

"I can't help that." He might as well berate me for breathing, I thought, wearily.

"No," he sighed again, "nor can I." He leaned forward and kissed me, gently, as if to wipe away the feel of Mendez' attack. "Sleep well, *mi jita*."

Chapter Five
The Commitment

As he moved away, it seemed as if the center of my world suddenly shifted, as well. It was the most disconcerting experience of my life. I grabbed his sleeve, anxiously. "I need the truth, Javier. What's going to happen to me?"

Javier was clearly nonplussed by the fear in my voice and he responded by jerking free, impatiently. "As soon as possible, I will take you to the border. After that, your fate is your own responsibility."

"And, until then?" I persisted.

He searched my face, as if he could find an answer in the fear I had revealed. "You will be under my protection," he answered, stiffly. "And I shall take greater care to see you are not harmed again."

"But how can you promise that if you go into battle?" I protested. I hadn't realized that Mendez had done far more damage with his words that with his hands. He had planted seeds of great uncertainty in the fertile ground of my confusion.

"Roberto will protect you," he insisted. "These men all know he would not hesitate to kill to protect me or my wife." He dismissed the subject and me with a sharp gesture.

"And...if you die?" I knew I shouldn't even think such a thing, much less blurt it out, but I had to know.

"Do you fear it?" he asked, turning back, slowly, his chin lifted mockingly. "Or do you pray for it?"

"I don't hate you, Javier," I said, shocked by the implication.

"Then why do you tremble at my touch?" he challenged, reaching out to caress my cheek and meeting quivering resistance. "Why do you pull away from me as though you find me repulsive?"

"I don't find you repulsive." I backed away from him, twisting my fingers together in agitation. His question was pushing me very close to a dangerous confession. "It's this. It's what you do that I find repulsive. It's what you want me to do." My lower lip trembled, giving me away. "It's not right, Javier. And you're lying to everyone who respects you and trusts you. I think Mendez already knows the truth. He told me there's a lot of talk about an American girl who left the same time you did, an American girl you brought back to your headquarters."

"Does it matter so much to you?" he asked, rubbing his eyes, wearily. "Is it so necessary that I tell everyone the truth?"

"It's necessary to tell me the truth," I said, looking at the floor. "If you expect to take my-" I stopped myself. "If you lie to your men then I know you will lie to a girl who has become an albatross around your neck."

It was clear he wanted to question me about the abrupt redirection of my words, but he paused, bewildered by my cliché. "Albatross? A bird? What has that to do with you or me?"

"Oh, you know," I answered, impatiently. "I'm nothing but trouble to you. I'm like a flapping, squawking weight around your neck...worthless."

"On the contrary, *mujer*," he drawled, his eyes doing that slow drop over my body that made me shiver and cringe at the same time, "you hold the promise of great worth." He dismissed the subject and me with a snap of his fingers. "I think I understand what you are saying. You cannot trust me to keep my word to you."

I nodded.

He shrugged. "What do I do? Do I tell these men the truth and let you suffer the penalty of my honesty?"

"There is no penalty for honesty," I said, sneering. "That's ridiculous."

"No? You do not have a saying..." he looked at me, piercingly, "the truth hurts?"

I sat down heavily. The truth would definitely hurt me.

"And the damage is done. Why should I tell them now? They would only demand their share of you." He leaned down to the end of the cot, and I drew back from him. He smiled and pulled up the blanket that had been left, folded, there. "Sleep, Dinah. Tomorrow we will find a solution so that you may feel safe in trusting me." He pulled the tent flap open. "Goodnight, Dinah."

I tugged the blanket around my shoulders and lay down. "Goodnight, Javier."

The battle raged all night. Not just in the tobacco fields, where darkness aided guerilla activities, but also in my nightmares. I couldn't escape the terrifying injuries, the brutal attacks, the piercing screams. I experienced them again and again.

I woke with the memory of the men in the bush near the village. I could still feel them, smell them, hear them. I was covered in perspiration and shaking in fear. I felt like a small child in fear of monsters in the closet, and I needed comfort and reassurance from any source. "Javier?" I whispered, searching the tent as my eyes became accustomed to the dark. I was alone.

I schooled myself against panic. He must be out checking the camp, I told myself, or heeding Nature's call, or something – anything. He'll be back. I sat up on the cot, and watched the door. He'll be back.

The night stretched on. I could hear movement of animals drawn to the smell of food, and the footsteps of sentries, patrolling the perimeter, the sizzle of a match strike as someone else waited out the night with a cigarette. I heard the first bird song of morning as the first streaks of sunlight breached the horizon. I heard the first stirrings of the camp kitchen, the first shot fired in the distance, and the answering shot and then a volley of shots and then the battle was on. Animals crept back into the jungle and soldiers rousted themselves and made ready for what could be the last battle they might fight.

And Javier never returned.

The tent flap fluttered and I looked up, hopefully.

A soldier entered, bring me a makeshift breakfast tray. "You eat, *Senora*," he said, setting the tray on the wooden crate in the middle of the tent, carefully keeping his eyes from mine as if I might bewitch him with a glance, and he might go mad and suffer the same fate as Mendez.

"Where is Jav-where is your captain?" I demanded. "Where is Roberto?"

The soldier shook his head and pointed at the tin tray.

"*¿Dónde están el capitán y Roberto?*"

He shrugged. "You eat, *Senora*." He made an exaggerated pantomime of eating.

"I'll eat," I promised, resignedly and reached for the cup of coffee at the edge of the tray. Yesterday I'd shared this cup with his commanding officer. Javier Enrique Diaz de Contreras, you're an arrogant and cold man, but you're all I've got at the moment. Funny, I used to have so much more and never realized it. I feel just like Dorothy in the Wizard of Oz. One moment, lounging on the patio at home, beneath a grape arbor casting a long cool shadow, and in a blink I'm at the middle of the world, in a musty, hot tent, my whole existence balanced on the humor of a man who is the very antithesis of everything I believe.

Right now, my father is probably trimming back the arbor for the year. I wonder if he can still hear me begging him not to destroy my childhood hideout? Does the patio smell like grape jelly and fresh baked bread? Is my cat, Duncan, curled up in a window, waiting for my return? Is the sky blue and endless and filled with the promise of freedom?

The tent flap moved again. I pushed the tray away, mindlessly, lost in a collage of wonderful and distant memories.

"It is a surprise and a pleasure to see you smile, Dinah," Javier said from the doorway.

I looked up, relief no doubt written over my face. He was clean shaven, and in a clean uniform. And he was back! "Oh." It was all I could manage to say.

He moved into the tent and dropped the flap back into place with a deliberate snap. "What were you thinking just now? What made you smile with such happiness?"

"I was thinking of home," I confessed, self-consciously running my fingers through my tangled hair. Who would have guessed he was such a good looking man under that beard and scowl?

Javier looked down at the tray beside me. "You did not eat. You are…what do you say…sick for home?"

When had we shifted so easily into speaking English all the time? "Homesick."

He ignored the correction. "You wish to be home?"

Home, with David and Julia and Duncan. Home, where I slept in clean sheets and silent streets? Home, where I would never have had an opportunity to help change lives, or…never met Javier? "Of c-course," I stammered. "If I had the choice, here is not where I would choose to be."

"But, you told me you came to this country of your free will," he reminded me, dropping to the canvas floor, one knee raised to support his chin.

"I chose to come here and help the sick and hungry," I retorted. It was hard to remember he was good looking when he was also so maddeningly right and so obviously aware of it. "Not to be held captive by a…a sex starved military puppet."

His eyes narrowed and he gestured toward the tent flap. "You are free to go, but I do not think you will get very far." He smiled. "As for sex-starved, if I understand you, I will soon have my fill of you. Did you not say you were here to feed the hungry?"

"Oh!" I turned away from him, feeling my face burn. "You disgust me."

He laughed at my flaming cheeks. "Your outrage is very charming, *mi jita*." He eased up to his haunches, to look at me, eye to eye. "But, I am not blind to the way you look at me with curiosity and desire. You wonder what it will be like to be loved by…" his brows pulled down in a frown, but there was a glimmer of something almost mischievous in his eyes, "sex-starved military puppet."

"Why, you-" I broke off the protest angrily. How dare he accuse me of such thoughts? How dare he think that I might be eager for his touch? How dare he be right?

"You will find out soon enough, *mujer*," he promised with an almost leering grin. His eyes slid over me. "Soon enough." He stood. "I shall send someone with hot water. Be certain to tie off the tent opening properly. I do not want anyone spying on you in your bath." He reached into a knapsack which seemed to have arrived in the tent at some time in the night because I did not recognize it. He held out a wonderfully familiar blue and white package.

"Ivory soap?" I said in disbelief. "Where did you get that?"

He shrugged. "It is a small passion of mine. It does not smell of lye or too sweet flowers as our local soaps do. I have a supply for my own purposes. And you," the smile returned, "are one of my purposes."

I wanted to fling the box back at him, but I didn't. The crude soap I'd been exposed to previously was foul smelling and sticky. To bathe in real soap again would be heavenly. I decided to ignore the fact that he had provided this toilette for his pleasure, not mine. "Thank you."

"*De nada*." He was whistling to himself as he left.

I lingered over the bath long after her pail of water grew cold. It felt so good to be clean again. I washed myself thoroughly, washed my hair, and then bathed all over again just for the pure joy of it. I was dressed in my clean slacks and shirt, drying my hair, and humming to myself when Javier returned.

I looked up from my task. "You could have knocked," I chided, "I might not have been dressed."

"That would not have stopped me," he answered. "You looked refreshed."

"I feel it," I agreed, brushing my hair.

Javier looked from me to the pail, where I was soaking my soiled clothing. "You are a remarkably practical woman, too. If I must be saddled with a woman in the middle of a battle, there could not be one more suited."

I smiled to myself. "Careful, Javier," I warned, "you nearly said something nice about me."

"I will say many nice things about you before this nice is over, no doubt." His voice held just the slightest hint of hunger. "Tonight you will not fight me." There was no query, nor was there warning. It was just a fact for him.

I shivered, yet I was not particularly frightened. "I'll try," I promised, biting my lip. "Only-"

"Roberto has been scolding me for bringing my wife into this place," he went on. "So I explained to him the facts. Now he scolds me for keeping you in a sin."

"Will he tell anyone?" I demanded anxiously, putting down my brush.

Javier shook his head. "He will not. I told him you were a modern American woman with *freedom*." He made the word a taunt. "You have your lovers as you choose."

Now was the time to make it clear to him I had never chosen. "Javier."

"Still he scolds me," Javier continued, as if unaware that I was speaking. "He says to me 'the girl loved her other men, how can she love someone who forces her?'" His eyes fell to search my face. He seemed to be disappointed that he didn't find denial in my expression. "Love is important to you?"

"Yes, I think it's important," I admitted in a whisper. "But, Javier, I-"

"So, I will make you a bargain." He held out his hand. "If you will love me enough not to fight me, I will not have to force you."

I stared at his outstretched hand. "You want me to love you?"

He nodded. "As you would your other lovers. We will both enjoy it more."

"But, what about you?" I felt a horrible lump growing in my throat, making it difficult to speak. "Will…will you love me?"

He shrugged carelessly. "What is love in the midst of so much death? Someone to hold in the night, nothing more. So…*si*, I will love you." His dark eyes tore away from me. "If I should live through this, I will no doubt, give my love to a woman who wants it for all time, a woman who will give me children."

"If?" I prompted.

He sighed heavily. "In the two days that I have been here I have seen many losses. There will be many more. These foolish people are stubborn," he said tightly. "They seek to wipe out a nation. There will not be many survivors."

"And you think you will die," I concluded, in a whisper.

"I am nearly certain of it." He didn't seem very distressed by this pronouncement. "So," he smiled grimly, "you will be my last love, yes?"

I shuddered. I could almost feel Death in that tent.

"Why do you look so sad, *mi jita*? Would you mourn me? Or do you fear for your own life? I will get you safely to the border, if I can," he promised.

"Your last love," I repeated.

He tapped my chin impatiently. "*Por favor,* do not bury me until I am dead. For now we will celebrate that I am very much alive."

I felt something...alien...a thrill that ripped through me. "When will you...?" I glanced down at the cot.

"Tonight. Roberto went to collect something for me." He smiled again.

I sat back and watched him. "You seem very pleased with yourself. Tell me, despite all you said about the war, does the battle go well at the moment?"

He looked down at me, thoughtfully. "Yes, it goes very well now."

After a supper of dried meat and refried beans, I sat on the ground near the fire, watching Javier review maps and mark sightings of small guerilla groups nearby. I couldn't help being struck by his ability to absorb a lot of information and transform it quickly into a reasonable course of action. And while he never looked at me or acknowledged me in any way, I knew he knew if any one of his men got too close to me. Every now and again his left hand would drift to his sidearm, and rest there, and suddenly a man would walk from behind me, getting out of my proximity swiftly.

When he was satisfied with the intelligence he had collected, he rolled up the maps and handed them to one of the men in the conference. He snapped his fingers as he approached me, and I sensed that I was supposed to jump up as any dutiful wife would be expected to do. While I resented it, I responded quickly and as soon as he was within reach, he took my hand and tucked it around his arm. We walked, arm in arm, toward the tent, followed by knowing and jealous looks and comments. I ignored them. All day I had conditioned myself for this moment and the waiting had become intolerable. I was eager to have it over.

Javier did not bother to light the oil lantern, but went directly to the cot and stretched out, before opening his arms for me to lie within them. He touched my face gently, caressed my shoulders and toyed with my hair as he spoke of his boyhood and rise in the military government. His stories were sometimes amusing, often touching and mostly horrifying, but he withheld little. It was as if he wanted me to know everything about him in just one night.

And he wanted to know about me, as well. He questioned me in detail about my home and family. He asked about my childhood, my dreams and plans. I tried to recount my favorite memories, but his casual touch was more than distracting.

Outside, it grew quiet. I must have fallen asleep in his arms for I woke to find him shifting over me, his body heavy and hard against me, his breath on my skin. I struggled with the urge to fight him. I might have given into my panic if there had not been a rustle at the tent flap, and Roberto's voice calling softly, "*Capitan?*"

"*Bueno.*" He shifted off me and the cot, and stood. He and Roberto exchanged a few words I could not hear, and then he turned and touched my shoulder. "Dinah."

I moved, slowly, bewildered. He was urging me upward and off the cot. Had he changed his mind? Had I been betrayed? Had something happened that had rearranged his plans? "Very well."

"Wait here," he whispered, leaving me standing alone in the center of the tent, but just as quickly he returned, with a hooded man beside him.

It was hard to make out any features but that ominous hooded shape. It was as if he had brought the Grim Reaper into the tent. "Javier, I don't understand."

"Do not fear, Dinah," he whispered. "This is Father Ocegueda. You saw him in the town, at his church, I'm sure." He tied the flap behind the man. "This can be the confessional, no?"

The hooded figure nodded.

Javier dropped to his knees, bowed his head and crossed himself. "Forgive me, Father, for I have sinned. It has been one year since my last confession."

I stared, open-mouthed, unable to reconcile this act of humility with the cruelty and arrogance I had seen at his hands. He spoke quickly, in such hushed tones I couldn't hear or understand what he was saying, which was only proper, since it was a confession. Suddenly, he lifted his head and sent a glance in my direction, as if to encompass me in his petition. "This woman, she is not my wife."

The priest's voice did not betray shock. "You are a man first, *Capitan*. You have carnal desires. You take what you want. Are you asking forgiveness for this sin of fornication?"

"My sin, Father, is that she is my wife in the eyes of my men, because I wanted to protect her. She is American, and my men are men first, too. She must not be passed around the camp like a bottle of wine. She must be taken, safely, to the border."

"I cannot take her tonight," the old priest said sadly. "I must make arrangements, contacts-"

"No, I will take her. I have given her my word that I would. But, I wish to have her – as you say…I am a man." There was a hint of anguish in his voice.

The priest reacted with shock at last. "You cannot ask me to condone such a sin," he protested.

"Nor can I die with such a sin," Javier interrupted. "Marry us tonight. She will be my wife in the eyes of God."

The priest looked at me. I could almost see his face now, and it might have been my own fancy, but he seemed to be imploring me to say no and to leave with him. "Do you agree to this?"

I looked from him to Javier, still on his knees, and back. This was so unexpected and out of character I wasn't completely certain that it wasn't just a dream. Or was it a trick? Perhaps just a costume drama to make me feel more willing, or did he actually care about my feelings? He was going to take what he wanted, regardless, but this effort to spare my feelings touched me more than anything any suitor had ever done before. "Yes," I said at last. "I agree."

Javier did not look at me, but I saw him nod to himself. Either he was pleased with his ruse, or pleased with me.

Roberto witnessed our vows, whispered quickly in Spanish, Javier translating for me. We knelt side by side, bodies not touching, until the priest asked, "By what symbol do you seal your pledge?"

Javier looked around the tent. "I have no ring," he said. "I will give her my cap." He pulled it from his head and settled it, almost reverently, on mine. "It is my greatest symbol of authority," he said solemnly.

The hat slipped down over my eyes, still warm from his touch. I should have laughed, it was so ludicrous, but I was moved by the sincerity in his pledge. He gave me something that meant more to him than the gold of any ring.

The priest blessed us, and moved to leave. "I will record the marriage tonight. The government might not acknowledge your marriage, but the Church will."

"*Gracias, Padre.*" Javier instructed Roberto to see the priest safely back to the edge of town.

Suddenly we were alone. I could actually feel the heat of his desire as he moved toward me. "Now," he said, his hands on my shoulders as if he thought I would try to run, "you are my wife. I possess you, and I am hungry for you." His hands slid up to my collar, and he began to pull my shirt away from my skin, his fingertips brushing each inch he exposed. "You would not fight your husband, would you, *mujer*?"

"No." My voice was hoarse and indistinct. I couldn't think clearly. He wanted me and I wanted him and it could be so wonderful, so much like all the romantic novels said it should, our first night as man and wife, if only…

"Please don't hurt me," I blurted as he eased me back onto the cot.

"Have no fear of me, Dinah," he muttered huskily as he pulled away his own clothing. "If you do not fight me, there is no need to hurt you." He touched my cheek with hot kisses while his hands roamed my body like a pirate counting his plunder.

Rationale was out the window at this point, but fear lingered. I'd never been fully aroused by a man before. In fact, I'd never allowed one to touch me this intimately. I'd heard horror stories, as well as romantic ones, regarding first encounters. I fidgeted beneath him. "Please, Javier." I begged.

He opened his eyes and looked down at me, and first there was anger, and then confusion. "Dinah," he demanded raggedly, "what do you want from me?"

"I…" How did I tell him? I couldn't. "Tell me what to do. I know it's going to hurt because I don't know what to do." It was a humiliating confession, and began to cry, and struggle to get away.

He rolled to his side, his arms tight around me so I could not get off the cot. "I do not understand. How could you not know what to do?" Suddenly his eyes widened. "You do not know because you have never done this before?"

I nodded, miserably, turning my face away, as tears fell. This wasn't me. I wasn't some lovesick girl or terrified virgin. I was a practical, intelligent woman – a nurse!

"You are a virgin?" he persisted.

That only made me cry harder, my tears spilling down on that hand that held me in place.

"*Madre de Dios,*" he breathed.

That completed my undoing. I twisted away from him, sobbing. "I'm sorry. I'm so sorry. I tried to tell you..." I didn't know why I was apologizing to him and that only made me feel worse.

"Yes, I knew you were scared but I thought that was because you felt it would be rape." He rolled away from me and climbed off the cot. Scrambling into his clothes, he avoided my eyes. "This is why you trembled when I touched you."

I struggled to sit up. "I wasn't asking you not to," I protested. "Just be patient with me."

"Be patient with you?" He laughed grimly. "Do I look as though I could be patient with you tonight? Look at me." He held out his hands. "I am shaking with anticipation. All day. All night. All I have been thinking about is you. Touching you, taming you, taking you. And you ask for patience! That is more torture than even I can bear. It would be better not to have you at all. Damn it," he swore, flinging my clothes at me, "dress yourself. I cannot stand to look at you."

I obeyed, biting down on my already swollen lip to stifle any other sound of pain or grief. Still a heartbroken sob escaped.

"Silence!" he commanded, keeping his back to me as he pulled on his boots. "It makes me insane to hear your voice – or your tears." He pushed open the tent flap.

"Where are you going?"

He looked back me in dark amusement. "Already you nag like a wife. Well, *mujer*," he snarled the title, "I'm going for a walk. A long walk."

I sat at the edge of the cot for a moment, my arms full of the clothing he had taken from me, trying to understand what had just happened. He had broken me down, inch by inch, bringing me to a place I had never imagined, to a place where I wanted nothing but his touch, and then he couldn't stand to look at me, hear me or touch me. His fury, his rejection were more violent and painful than if he had just raped me that first day and left me behind.

I dragged the shirt across my face to dry my tears, and tugged my slacks on. I had to find him and try to make something out of this holy mess we had made.

I got to the tent flap, half dressed, frantic, and froze. I was actually running after him, begging him. I had never chased after a man in my life. I certainly wasn't going to chase after *him* – even if he was my husband in the eyes of the Church.

I stood there in the doorway, searching the darkness. To my right, a figure moved and I turned, hopefully.

It was only one of the soldiers. This one was young, pale, and skinny, returning naked from the latrine. As he passed our eyes met and locked, filled with curiosity. For a moment, I was so miserable that it was tempting to call him back to the tent and let him finish the task Javier found so distasteful. The temptation passed almost before it crystalized and instead of acknowledging him further, I pulled back into the tent and let him pass, disappearing into the darkness.

I dropped down onto the cot and looked around the tent made so empty by Javier's absence. What am I supposed to do? I wondered. Tears welled again and I blinked hard to prevent them falling. I had to regain control, and be strong. But…the truth was I wanted my Daddy.

In my entire life, there had never been a problem I couldn't bring to my father, David. When I was small, he bravely slew the dragons that hid in my closet. When I was an adolescent, and feeling awkward and uncomfortable with my changing body, it was my father who sat down with me, and with no small amount of stammering and blushing, somehow got through the facts of life without hedging on any detail. And after that, it was my father who was brave enough to trust me implicitly. When a boy got too pushy on a date, I went to my father for advice. Somehow he managed to restrain his desire to break legs and let me handle the situation myself.

It wasn't that Janice was in any way lacking as a mother, but I had always been Daddy's Little Girl. Now, as much as I longed for David's advice, I would have been ashamed for either of them to see me; half-dressed and abandoned in a stranger's tent, somewhere in the middle of a foreign country's war-torn jungle. I could imagine my mother wringing her hands, her smooth brow furrowed up in pain, a soft, "Oh, Dinah," escaping her trembling lips in an anguished sigh. David wouldn't frown, he wouldn't wring his hands or sigh. He wouldn't shout, preach, threaten or curse, either. He'd stand there, stoically, with a half-smile meant for support, and a hand held out to help, but there would be no mistaking that single tear slipping down his cheek.

"Oh, Daddy," I whispered, flinging myself down on the cot. "I never meant to make you cry."

At some point, when exhaustion made my lungs burn and my eyes were nearly swollen closed, I must have drifted into a troubled sleep. There was no rest, however, for I was chased through the night by demons of my own creation. Lost in a steamy, swampy jungle, where the trees dripped vividly colored snakes, with long, flicking, pointed tongues that raked over my bare skin as I ran, my bare feet burned by hot ground, my legs and body stung by vines that caught and tore at my flesh, trying to hold me back, and enormous multicolored insects that bit my back and breasts viciously.

As I ran, I called out, first, I thought, for my father, but then I realized it was Javier with whom I was pleading. Suddenly, the swampy underbrush cleared and I found myself in the center of a hundred men, trying to cover myself as they laughed and pointed and jeered.

I begged and cried and began to scream as the men encircled me, moving closer and closer until I was engulfed by gruel, groping hands. I pushed, and swatted and kicked and bit, but they wrestled me to the ground and pinned me, spread-eagled on the scorching earth.

Suddenly, the crowd parted and, except for those four men who held me down, I was left alone, crying and staring up at a steamy yellow sky. A shadow passed over the sky and I saw black eyes staring down me, black eyes filled with contempt and anger.

"Javier," I cried, bucking and struggling to free myself.

He stood over me, hands on hips, watching in grim amusement. Beside me, one of the men, with a toothy leer, looked up. "You want her?" he offered.

Javier's brows rose, disdainfully. "Her?" he said, nudging my thigh with the toe of a highly polished boot. "Not her," he spat, and strode away.

I began to scream again, but my throat had closed up and my screams remained silent in my dreams.

Chapter Six
The Communion

Roberto came back with the first fingers of dawn. "*Senora,*" he called softly.

"No, Javier," I moaned, still half asleep.

"*Senora*, he is not in camp," Roberto whispered reassuringly. "Wake up."

I rolled onto my back, rubbing my burning eyes. When I finally focused on the man leaning over me, I was acutely aware of my half-dressed state, and I sat up, tugging my shirt up to cover me.

Roberto was frowning as he backed away from me. His eyes went all around the tent in the dim light, unable to look at me. "Was it...was it so terrible?" he asked in a voice that seemed filled with guilt.

I twisted away from him, embarrassed, fighting back more tears. "It was awful," I confessed in a whisper.

Roberto's hand jerked toward me, pulled back and finally reached my bare shoulder, where he patted me, awkwardly. "Poor *nina,*" he said.

"Where is he?" I asked when I could speak without fear of wailing. How could he leave me? How could he abandon me after he went through that charade with the priest? Oh, was it only a charade? My humiliation was just as raw and black in the morning as it had been the night before.

Roberto let his hand drop and he shook his head. "He left very early. I think he goes..." He pointed in the direction of the tobacco fields.

"Oh, no." Beyond the humiliation was a different sensation, one just as powerful and just as painful. It was fear. If he had returned to the battlefield, he might die. And I would be a widow who never had never known her husband's lovemaking...or his love.

"Wait." Roberto went to the tent and peered out. "You must be packed and ready to go when he returns tonight."

"To the border?" He was awfully eager to get rid of me now, wasn't he?

He shrugged again.

I looked down at my hands, knotted up in the fabric of my borrowed shirt. He must very incredibly angry to be so determined to get me to the border now, even when it will mean crossing battle lines to do so.

"To go tonight means not to suffer again," Roberto pointed out.

"Suffer?" I repeated, wretchedly. "He *married* me."

Roberto nodded as if he understood. He patted my shoulder again. "If he should live, he would not follow you. He would…" he pantomimed something and when I didn't respond he did it again. It looked as if he were tossing a basketball in the air…or a bird.

"He would set me free?" I guessed. I knew that. Roberto thought he was comforting me, but the ephemeral state of the relationship only saddened me. If we did not feel love for one another, we had cheapened the institution of marriage. He had said he would save his true love for a woman who would love him the way he wanted – no, expected to be loved, a woman who would give him children. And if I did love him, I had wasted myself on a man who could not love me. "I know," I said, nodding. "I know."

Roberto nodded, too. "I bring coffee," he promised and left me.

"Thank you." I got up and dressed, and began to tidy up the cot, arranging the pillow, smoothing out the rumpled blanket. Something green and heavy fell to the canvas floor with a metallic clatter. I knelt and fumbled under the cot gingerly. It was the green, billed cap that he had so reverently placed on my head the night before. I knew I had no right to wear it, so I put it on the pillow of the cot.

How naked he must feel without it, I mused, and how glad he will be to reclaim it.

Roberto brought the coffee, as promised. I was very glad to accept it. "*Gracias*. You are very kind to me."

He blushed and bowed a little. "With a man like the *Capitan*..."

I realized with a jolt that Roberto was embarrassed by the way I had been treated. "He's had a hard life," I said, quickly. "His father was taken away by the government when he was a baby. His mother was r-raped and killed by bandits before his eyes. He doesn't dare care for anyone anymore."

Roberto's blush darkened. It was clear he knew these things and did not like to hear them spoken aloud. I wondered, for a moment, if Roberto had been some kind of family servant before Javier joined the military. "Perhaps," he began slowly, "for a woman like you...."he shook his head. "I am old fool." He turned away to leave.

Something about his demeanor alarmed me. "Roberto?" I risked putting a hand on his arm. "What is it? What is wrong?"

Roberto looked around, hesitantly, and then lowered his voice to a whisper. "You must vow before God not to speak of this – to anyone."

"Of course," I agreed.

He waited, watching me.

I put a hand up and repeated, "I swear before God that I will never speak of this to anyone."

Satisfied, he inched a bit closer. "The government…it is bad. Very bad. Worse than before. Javier knows this, in his heart, but I do not think he knows here." He touched his temple. "You know it. Your government. You have sent ships and guns to help the rebels. The government cannot last. If it fails, the army will fail, too."

It took me a minute to fully grasp the significance of his words. "No," I whispered. "You think my government will destroy this army? Javier will be a war criminal. They will put him in prison …or worse." I pressed fingertips to the bridge of my nose to prevent more tears.

Roberto nodded. "*Padre* Ocegueda says there is already a price on his head. Oh, do not worry, *Senora*, you will be safe in America. These rebels will not dare harm you."

"Perhaps not, but what about…" both of us turned to look at the cap on the bed, "my husband?"

"No, no, Senora, do not think of it. He married you to die with a clean soul. You cannot grieve for a heart he does not have and you must not give him yours."

I sighed. I knew the old man was right, and yet…

"Excuse me. I have duties."

"Roberto?"

He turned from the tent flap.

"Perhaps, Javier could come with me-"

He shook his head adamantly "He will not desert his men, no matter how hopeless this has become. Not even for you."

"But, he is condemning himself to death!"

"Perhaps, for him, that is easier than living." He paused. "He says you might have done the same thing to come here in this time." He pulled the tent flap back and hurried out before I could ask another question.

Javier returned sooner than I had expected. Roberto led me to believe he wouldn't return until after dark, but there he was striding around camp just after the noon meal, while I was looking after the soldiers in the camp infirmary. He looked hot and dusty and very tired, yet oddly pleased. He gestured for me to return to the tent, and I went, obediently, unreasonably glad to see him.

Inside the tent, I perched on a wooden crate, feeling that going to the bed might make one or both of us uncomfortable. To my surprise, he dropped to the floor beside me. "*Buenos dias, Senora,*" he said, lazily, dragging his sleeve across his brow.

"Buenos dias," I answered, hoping that I didn't give away just how happy I was that he had returned. It appeared, however, that he did not want to discuss it. "Is the battle going well?"

"Hmm?"

I turned toward him. He was staring at me, but I doubt he was seeing me. He had a faraway look about him. "The battle?" I prompted.

"Yes." His eyes seemed to come back into focus. "It is…I do not wish to discuss it now. Did Roberto tell you we will travel tonight?"

I nodded, and his cap slid down over my eyes.

He pushed the cap up again, started to speak, shifted his attention to the tent flap, listening intently for a moment, and then whispered, "As soon as night has fully fallen. I do not want our departure to be marked."

"Do you think we'll get to the border tonight?" I asked, matching his hushed tone.

He eased himself upward, reaching up to adjust the cap that no longer sat on his head. He frowned, lowered his hand, and then shrugged. "We will get where we wish to be tonight," he answered cryptically.

I wanted to ask questions, get clarification, but he strode out of the tent with purpose. I got up and followed as far as the door, watching him march out into the middle of the encampment. He seemed too tall, too strong, too powerful to be destroyed by a mere wicked government, and yet I knew my fear was a real one. I suppose I should have been frightened for myself, if something happened to

Javier – and it seemed inevitable that it would – but a strange new fear was taking over. If something happened to Javier, nothing else would matter.

I pulled away from the tent flap and returned to the wooden crate. How could a man cause such feelings in a woman? How could such a man make *me* feel that way?

Could it be as simple as the word husband? It was not a word I have ever thought I would use possessively. I'd only ever thought about being strong, independent, useful; I'd always seen myself as one of those tiny candles faithfully lit in darkness. I never believed I would have time for a husband and children for many years, if ever – not when there were so many poor and hungry children in the world.

Now the choice had been made for me, at least as far as a husband was concerned. I would not turn my back on Javier unless he ordered me to, and then it would be a struggle between duty and...and what? What amazing affliction of my powers of reason existed in this oppressive jungle heat? I wiped my brow and pushed the billed cap back on my face, just in time to see Javier return to the tent.

"You must rest now, *mi jita.* You will get none tonight." Just for a moment a smile flickered across his face. Was he really so happy to be rid of me?

He had gestured toward the cot so I rose and went to it, obediently. I wanted to be happy, too. I wanted to rejoice and be relieved that I was going home to my parents and my life, but his cavalier manner of discarding me hurt.

It must have shown in my face for, as I knelt on the bed, arranging the pillow and blanket, he touched my hand. "Are you well? Just now Roberto ..." he paused for a moment, "scolds?"

I nodded. "Scolded."

"Scolded me for leaving you to suffer this morning."

I knew it. I knew Roberto, far from the quiet, obedient and loyal man he acted, would speak his mind if he felt something was wrong. "I'm fine," I promised. His eyes felt warm on me and it made me uncomfortable. It was too intimate, too possessive.

"I know I was harsh on you last night, Dinah, and I also know it was not your fault." He reached out to flick away a bit of dust that clung to my cheek. "When I left you, I was so angry I wanted to run through the camp screaming and shooting. But, I could not, of course, so I walked. I walked a long way. As I walked I realized that I should be...flattered?"

I didn't react. Flattered? Could he have chosen a more demeaning word?

"...that you were so willing under the circumstances. I am glad you told me the truth. It could have been..." he paused again and looked around. "The first time for a girl can be difficult, painful if a man is not careful."

My mouth was dry and my head pounded in my temples. I tried to swallow, but there was a lump in my throat. "Thank you for understanding," I said with difficulty. "I was afraid."

"I do not believe that." To my surprise, he was laughing. "You are never afraid. You are ...*audaz*." He made a fist. "Bold." He relaxed his fingers. "And the night is over so there is nothing to fear." He urged me backward on the cot. "Rest, Dinah. We have a long journey ahead of us."

I didn't know how I could find a moment's peace to rest and yet, when Javier touched my cheek again, I opened my eyes to find that the tent was completely dark.

"Dinah," he whispered, "it is time to go."

I sat up groggily. "My things..."

"I have arranged everything." He took my hand and pulled me to my feet. "Let us go."

I stepped outside and found two soldiers at the corner of the tent. Startled, I turned and accusing stare at Javier, who nodded. "*Vamonos*," he said.

I followed them, as I was urged to do, and Javier fell in behind. I had to admit that I was scared. Was this the carefully staged ploy I had been expecting? Was the trap I feared real, after all? Of course, not, I argued. He's had many opportunities to be rid of me before this. He had no need to follow me when I left the camp, or to rescue me when I was attacked. There had to be a reason for leaving in this manner, yet, I couldn't help but be aware of his steps behind me, and sensed every movement with dread.

"I would not be so foolish as to travel under these circumstances alone, *mujer,*" he said suddenly, as if he could hear my thoughts. "These men I can trust to accompany us, and we will need them later, as well."

I didn't answer, I just kept walking, but my mind was spinning. Were we going to the border? Then why didn't we take all of my things? If we aren't going to the border, then where exactly are we going? I felt my stomach churning with anxiety.

"Do you trust me, Dinah?" he challenged quietly.

"I have to," I answered tightly. Do I? I wondered for what must have been the hundredth time since I found myself being muscled up to his bedroom back in the town. Can I trust him? He has made himself my husband, but what does that mean to him? What does it mean to me, really?

I didn't realize the question had stalled all processes until he tapped me on the shoulder. "Keep moving, Dinah, this is no time to delay."

I began to walk again, no more certain than I was before.

"It will be all right soon, Dinah," he said softly. "I promise."

I felt the tension inside me ease, if not ebb away. Having Javier as my husband meant that he would mean all that a husband should mean to a woman. I stopped again, with a gasp.

"What is wrong? What happened?" He wrapped his arm around me, his voice anxious. "Did something sting you? Are you injured?"

"No, no. I'm fine. I'm sorry." I squirmed out of his arms and stumbled forward, stunned. I loved him. I wanted him. And I was willing to trust him.

I don't know how far we walked, but by my calculations, we had walked for just over an hour – not brisk walking but not a casual stroll, either. I would have estimated about three miles, but I had no evidence to support it. I did know we had walked mostly north, and had climbed up a slight grade. Based on my limited knowledge of the country, and what I had seen back at the camp, I was preparing myself for another four or five hours of travel.

Therefore, I was surprised when Javier moved ahead of me suddenly and signaled for our guards to stop. We were in a clearing, and somewhere nearby water was rushing – lots of it, so it must be a river, or perhaps we were closer to the coast than I realized. I couldn't smell the sea air, but I could smell night blooming flowers from somewhere very nearby. Javier muttered some instructions to one of the men, who moved away with a lantern, blacked out on three sized. I could see the path of yellow light for a while, but eventually, it disappeared into the darkness.

Javier found a log for me to rest on, and I sat, staring up at the black sky, trying to find constellations to help me map where I was. There were so many stars, I couldn't pick out the ones I needed.

The soldier returned, far sooner than I expected, breaking a silence so loud I wanted to scream just to fill it up. He walked up to Javier and nodded. "*Si, Capitan,*" was all he said. His curious black eyes rested on me for a moment, but his face remained as impassive as stone.

Javier turned toward me, one hand extended to me, the other accepting a canvas pack from the second soldier. "Come, *mi jita.*"

I got up and followed after him, uncertainly. The first soldier lit another lamp in the same fashion as the one he had used, and offered it to me, along with a bedroll. The soldiers did not follow us as Javier moved away from the clearing. I stumbled along behind him, wondering what he was thinking, to leave our security team behind. I stopped and glanced over my shoulder. The other lamp was moving back in the direction we'd come. We were now alone.

"This way." Javier touched my sleeve, making me jump.

The path was no longer smooth or solid. Suddenly it was a struggle to remain upright. My feet kept slipping out from under me. Where was he going? "Oh!" Suddenly I was face down on a moss covered path of rocks.

"Watch your step," he hissed, helping me up and guiding me over a small, trickling of inky water. "Just ahead are *cascadas*...water..."

"Waterfalls," I breathed, staring. Even in the blackness of night, the silver white water spilling from nothingness into infinity was breathtaking.

He moved up behind me. "One of the most famous geographic features of our country, and behind them is a cave," he said, reminding me of a tour guide.

The tone irritated me. This wasn't Disneyland. This was a stifling jungle night, filled with mystery, beauty and fear and the uncertainty of my life was hanging in a balance I couldn't even see. "Yes?"

"So," there was a smile in his voice, "that cave is very cool and very private." He moved ahead of me, swinging the lantern back and forth to give me fleeting views of the area around the waterfalls.

"So?" I repeated, but suddenly I understood, as if a neon light had appeared over his head. I stopped struggling on the slippery path and stared at his back. I started to giggle.

He stopped walking and looked down at me, swinging the lantern toward me. "What is so funny?" he demanded.

"You're taking me on a honeymoon," I laughed.

"It is the American custom, is it not?" he pointed out.

"Yes, it is. I just didn't expect it from you, from this situation." I gestured toward the water. "It's practically the Amazonian Hilton!"

"The Amazon river is not in El Salvador," he said, indignantly.

I huffed in frustration. "Yes, but-"

"But, what? I married an American. There are certain customs I can respect. Does this displease you?" he challenged.

"No, but-"

"No more arguments." He came down the path just enough to reach out for my hand. "We're nearly there."

I let him take my hand. His skin was hot against mine. He was anxious. My heart went out to him a little more. I would not remind him that the night before he had no concern for such conventions.

We had reached the plateau, and the mist of the rushing water floated over us, cooling us instantly. It roared around us. It swallowed us. He moved close to me and raised his voice to be heard. "This is the first time for you. It may be painful. You may cry out."

I turned around sharply.

"But I will try to be careful," he added, pulling me toward the water.

I resisted, but he continued to pull me toward the sheets of water pounding the pool below. As we reached the pool's edge, he let the lantern's light play on the water, revealing a small opening in the torrent, created by a jutting rock. Balanced on small boulders at the edge of the water, we slipped through the curtain of water, and inside the cave.

He hooked the lantern on an exposed root, and put the bedroll down on the ground.

"Why here, Javier?"

"I thought I had explained that to you," he said, not looking up at me. "It is private." He gestured broadly. "No sounds will be penetrate these walls to reveal your…" he paused, glanced up and resumed his task, "status to others."

"Oh, so this was to keep up the pretense at the camp." I was actually a little disappointed.

He didn't appear too concerned that he might have hurt me. "If you prefer to think that, you may. I thought you might be more comfortable without so many ears nearby."

I licked my lips, watching the precise way he laid out our bridal bed. "I suppose, then, I am grateful," I conceded, but his explanation had stolen the touch of magic from the place.

His hands stilled and he frowned at the bedroll. "I was not seeking gratitude, Dinah," he murmured. He flicked another glance at me. "I wanted it to be apart from the circumstances that brought us together. I do not want your memories of such an event to be clouded by gunfire and bloodshed."

I sighed, feeling both ungrateful and deeply moved. Even working his way so carefully around the facts of the situation, his words made me tingle with unexpected anticipation and shyness. "Thank you, Javier."

He nodded and stood. "Come here, *Senora* Contreras," he commanded softly.

I obeyed on rubbery legs.

He reached out and drew me closer. "Come to me, Dinah, don't be afraid." His touch was gentler than it had ever been.

He touched my cheeks, cupping my face between his hands, gazing deeply into my eyes, as if to memorize every aspect of the soul revealed there. "You have such soft skin, Dinah." He seemed to breathe my name. "Everywhere I touch is like satin, cool and smooth and giving." One hand slid down my chin to my throat. "Relax, Dinah, this is right." He smiled encouragingly as his fingertips toyed with the lobe of my ear.

I trembled. I was confused. I was frustrated by his motives, hungry for his touch.

"After I left you last night, I walked here. I knew this place as a retreat in my youth and I realized there was no more fitting place to have you this." His hands fell to the collar of my shirt and he eased the buttons away swiftly. "We will have the serenade of waters and the flowers will stand guard for us." He smiled, pushed the shirt away and expertly unhooked my bra. "You see? I can be romantic if I try."

I didn't care. He could have been giving me economic forecasts and it would have seemed lyrical to me as his hands slid over my exposed skin. I caught my breath as his fingers moved forward and cradled my breasts.

"Do not be afraid, Dinah," he repeated. "I give my word to treat this as sacred." His fingers tightened around my nipples and I gasped in surprise and pleasure. "Do I hurt you?"

"Oh, no!" If he had I had never felt such exquisite pain in my life. I no longer feared the consequences my recent decisions had delivered to me. I only wanted to make love with him. "Javier, please," I moaned as he lowered his mouth to replace his fingers.

His laugh became something deep and animalistic, and he stepped back to start pulling our clothing away. When we were both naked, he stared at me in the faint golden light of the lantern. He was breathing with difficulty, and there was no doubt, even in my limited understanding, that he wanted me. "Now, Dinah."

"Now, Javier." I let him pull me down onto the bedroll.

"This makes you mine, Dinah Contreras," he said, his hands sliding and stalling over my body, as if trying to memorize every curve and plane. "No matter what happens tomorrow, or the day after, or whatever your life brings, where it takes you when you leave me, you will be mine. No other man will ever know you the way I know you."

"There will never be another man, Javier," I vowed. There could never be another man, not now.

His lips found mine with even more urgency. "Yes, Dinah," he whispered fervently when he tore his mouth from mine. "There will be another man. I demand it. There is too much life in you to mourn me when this is over."

His words hurt more than any physical thing he could do to me. "Oh, but Javier, you're my-"

"It does not matter." He dismissed the fact of our marriage with a terse decree, but he must have seen the pain in my eyes because he kissed my brow, gently. "Our marriage for tonight, *querida*. Fate demands it that way. Tomorrow we will go to the border and you will be taken away from me. You will go home. And I will go, I think, to my death. You must marry again...and on that occasion, a man who will better suit you." He frowned, but it wasn't an angry expression. "Choose wisely, Dinah. Choose a man worthy of you, of your great faith and noble heart."

"Javier," I insisted, quietly, "I have chosen."

He shook his head. "You did not choose, I chose for you. And I selfishly chose for you a husband with no tomorrow. Listen to me," he chided as I looked away. "I forbid you to dress your heart in widow's rags for the rest of your life because of some..." he glanced around the darkness, "romantic notion." He brushed my cheek tenderly. "Tell me you will marry again."

I pulled away and sat up, covering myself, self-consciously.

"Dinah?"

I looked down at him. He cared about me. It was obvious that he did. His feelings might not transcend to the level of my own, he might not ever love me as I understood love, but he did care and, perhaps, I could play on those feelings. "But, what if you don't die?"

"I would not make it difficult for you," he promised. "There is no record of our marriage going to the United States, except right here." He touched my breast.

Impulsively, I moved my hand to entwine our fingers and hold his hand there. "I don't want you to die, Javier," I pleaded.

He shrugged as if my plea was meaningless. "It is a choice I made long ago. Perhaps, if I had known…" he smiled at me, "I might have chosen differently. But, Dinah, I have chosen. "Even if I should continue to breathe on this earth, I should think myself dead – and you must do the same. There is no tomorrow for us, Dinah. Do you understand?"

No, I didn't understand, but a dozen possibilities assailed me. "Are you already married? I mean, to someone else?"

He seemed repulsed by the idea that I could even think such a thing. "No. Of course not. I confessed before a priest."

"Are you engaged to someone else?"

He shook his head. "No, Dinah, before you, I had never considered marriage, at least, not for a very long time, and there was no particular woman I wanted or respected enough to marry."

This mollified me somewhat, but I still didn't understand. "Then why do you insist that I forget you and marry someone else? If you do not die, then I am not free to marry anyone else."

"I promise you, if I do not die, I will seek an annulment, and then you will be free. So go home and find a man to love for the rest of your life." He pulled himself up beside me, hugging his knees, his shoulder pressing against mine to turn me toward him. "I have given you my promise, Dinah, now I want yours." He leaned toward me and kissed me.

If I had believed, even for a moment, that I could have forgotten him and moved on to another man, that belief was ash in my heart. Nothing could have survived the fire he set with that kiss. I twisted against him, my arms around his neck, and returned the kiss with all the desire and desperation in my body.

He broke the kiss after a moment, holding me back enough that he could meet and study my eyes. "Do I have your promise, Dinah? I will stop now, if you will not promise."

"No," I sobbed, "don't stop."

"Promise me." His fingers tangled in my hair as he pulled me down. "Promise me, Dinah." He kissed me again. "I will go no further until I have your word," he whispered against my mouth.

"I can't promise," I wept, clutching at him, trying to make every inch of him touch every inch of me. "I can't simply blot you out of my memory. I can't forget this. I never will."

He pulled away, sharply, and began to gather his clothes together.

I watched him, stunned and hurt. "What are you doing? Where are you going?"

"Back," he answered tightly.

"'Back'?" I echoed. "Back where?"

"To the camp." He pushed clothing at me.

"Why?" I grabbed his shirt and held it. "Why are we going back? What's wrong?"

"Everything," He tugged at the shirt and when I resisted, he sagged in defeat. "For you, Dinah. I cannot imprison you in a memory. If you cannot accept tonight for what it is, I will not torture you tomorrow, and all the tomorrows to come."

"Javier," I begged, "please. Please, I can't bear to hear you talk about tomorrow that way."

"Very well, *mi jita*." It was clear that leaving went against everything he believed in, everything he wanted, and he capitulated in palpable relief. "Will you promise?" He pulled me close to him. "Not because I want to be cruel, but because I cannot bear for Fate to be cruel to you."

I nodded against him, my face pressed hard against his neck. It was a lie. I would never forget him.

"You are a remarkable woman, Dinah McKee de Contreras," he sighed, satisfied.

He stretched out on the bedroll and encouraged me to lie down next to him. "Dios, you are lovely to look at," he declared at last. "I could gaze on you without ceasing, I could drink in your beauty until I never thirsted again. Eyes like sky, hair like early corn, a body that would spoil a man for any other woman. I have wanted to possess you from that first time I saw you – a lifetime ago."

His hands played over me as if I was a finely tuned instrument and he was a maestro. He brought me to dizzying crescendos of need with his nearness. He murmured promises of fulfillment I had never comprehended until that moment in his arms. It was as if, suddenly, Shakespeare had come alive, as if the marvelous transitions of spring had been defined for me. He created colors for me alone, he played notes only I could hear, he made a world, an existence, in which only we could ever live.

"You belong to me, Dinah," he growled into my hair. "You are mine at this moment and for all eternity. Say it, Dinah," he commanded. "I want to hear you say it."

"Take me, Javier. I am yours."

Chapter Seven
The Capitulation

The battle had overrun the camp by the time we returned. Javier had sent the two soldiers ahead and as we neared the encampment, we could hear the static fire of machine guns.

Javier's hand tightened around mine, and he cursed under his breath.

I looked up at him. To be truthful, my world, my awareness was centered on him at that moment, and the reality of what was ahead of us just didn't register with me, but his darkly sorrowful expression told me all. "I'm glad we had last night, Dinah," he said, grimly, "but it will not ease my regret for today."

He released my hand and marched ahead, leaving me to follow, woodenly. That morning, I had awakened from my wedding night to find my new husband crouching on the ground near the roaring blue water, listening intently to something I only marginally recognized as distant gunfire. It was a shock, a crude and cruel one.

Javier had abruptly gestured for me to dress and pack and I complied swiftly, despite my complaining body. As we approached the curtain of water, he surprised me by abruptly taking me in his arms and kissing me deeply and passionately. Then, just as abruptly, he released me and we left the cave.

He stopped several hundred feet beyond the camp's perimeter and held up a hand. "You will wait here, *mi jita*," he commanded, without looking back at me. He lowered his hand and eased his gun from its holster. He examined it briefly and handed it to me. "If anyone approaches you, shoot to kill."

I took the gun with trembling fingers. I believe that I had earned his respect, and possibly his affection, and I wasn't going to lose it by acting like a ninny now.

His fingers closed around mine as I took the weapon. "It is all right to be frightened, Dinah," he told me, still not looking at me. "I, too, am frightened." He looked toward the sounds of battle. "For the first time in my life, I am frightened." He released my hand and walked away.

"*Vaya con Dios*," I called after him. He paused, nodded, and continued his stealthy approach to the camp. I watched him go and in my heart, I was going with him. The night before had been more than the completely of a physical act, it had been the completion of the joining we had made before a priest and a witness, essentially before God. I was, and forever would be, a part of him.

Once he was out of sight, I searched the area where he'd left me, seeking a place where I could sit, out of the blazing sun, out of sight of anyone moving along the path. I found a rock a few feet from the broken grass. It was partially shaded by low level branches of a llama tree. I didn't know much about the fruit, except that it had a short season, which had already passed, and the flesh was mild in flavor and was stringy. I had been introduced to the pink fleshed llama when I first arrived here, and found it a bit too tart for my tastes, but I would have been grateful for it that day.

For hours, I sat as still as I could, listening to gunfire and screaming, sometimes so close it made me cringe and then, suddenly, inexplicably, it grew silent. It stayed silent, broken only occasionally by a single gunshot. But, the silence did not bring Javier back to me.

By nightfall, he still had not returned, and I was weak, frightened and close to succumbing to an alien despair I'd never encountered in my entire life. It was not humanly possible for someone to remain so quiet and still for so long. I was beginning to contemplate unspeakable actions if Javier did not return by morning. Just about the time I had resolved to do something to end my suffering, I heard a rustling near me, and I froze.

"Dinah?" It was a soft, urgent whisper, but I recognized it. I couldn't make my voice work to express my relief. I just let the tears fall, unchecked. "Dinah?" There was anguish in his voice now. "Please, answer."

"I…I'm here," I croaked at last.

Javier emerged from the bushes on the other side of the path, the moon on his skin made him look pale and worn. "You're hurt!" I cried, trying to climb down the rock even though every muscle and joint in my body resisted.

He was at my side in an instant, his hands, holding me still. "We must get away from here," he said hoarsely. "We will follow the troops to the North." He leaned forward against the rock, his head hanging low between his shoulders. "We must get you to the border."

The moonlight spilled onto the bloody, ragged hole in his pants. "You're hurt," I gasped.

He straightened, as if ashamed to be seen weak or in pain. "Nothing to worry about," he cut in. "It's not safe to be here. The rebels are moving by night. They…" his voice dropped as if he couldn't catch his breath. "They ambushed my men in their sleep. I should have been there."

I staggered under a wave of guilt. Once again, I had been the reason men had died.

"No, Dinah." He touched my chin, drawing my face upward. "I am grateful to God you were not there. Now, come."

I followed him, nearly running, his gun pressing against my side where I had tucked it into the waistband of my pants. "Javier," I gasped, as I caught up to him, "Where is Roberto?"

He stopped, tipping his head up as if to search the Heavens.

I followed his gaze. "Oh, Javier."

He began to run again. "We will go back to the cave tonight. It is the only place we might sleep safely." He didn't admit that he no longer thought he could get to the border in his state, but was panting as he moved, clearly growing weaker. "We will rest and eat and tomorrow we'll find a way through the rebel lines to get you out of the country."

"Let me look at your leg," I pleaded. "Please, it will only take a moment, but you might not make it back to the cave, otherwise."

He capitulated almost thankfully, even though he scowled as he sank onto a fallen log. "It is only grazed," he insisted as I tore the fabric away, sticky with blood.

"It's a gunshot wound," I said, shocked.

He gestured weakly. "What would you expect from a gun battle?" He tried to smile. "What is it you say…you should see the other guy?"

I tore the damaged cloth into strips, trying not to dwell on what that remark implied. "It looks as if it went all the way through. I've got antiseptic in my bag." I reached for it, relieved that it had not been forgotten in the fray. "I can clean and cover it, but that's the best I can do.

Javier's eyes were closed as he leaned back, waiting for me to perform such ministrations. His pallor was frightening and I had to force myself to keep my eyes off his face as I worked. I could not panic now. I needed my strength and presence of mind. Most of all, I needed Javier. "There," I said, at last. "Now we'll just pray for the best."

Javier did not react.

"Javier?" My voice rose slightly, but urgently. "Javier?"

He moved, but did not open his eyes.

He's passed out, I realized, resting my head against the log where he sat. What now? I can't move him and we can't stay here. I glanced at the canteen at his waist. Could it still contain some of the brandy he had brought away from the head-quarters back in town? I reached for it and tugged it from the loop on his belt. Twisting it open, I had to send a small prayer of gratitude Heavenward that it was not empty, and I raised it to his barely parted lips.

He choked and spluttered, but his eyes flew open and focused on me, jerking the canteen from my fingers. "*Por el amor de Dios,* are you trying to drown me?" he snapped.

I sat back on my haunches. "You passed out," I answered. At least he was his usual arrogant self.

He snatched the canteen cap from my fingers and screwed it into place. "Let us go."

I stood and offered him a hand, but he pushed it away and struggled to stand and start walking under his own power. "We are not too far from the cave," he insisted, through gritted teeth and he tried not to wobble. "Can you hear the water?"

I followed, shouldering my bag, wondering what I'd done this time to make him angry this time. No one would ever mistake this for a conventional marriage, I thought with a sigh.

He glanced over his shoulder. "I suppose you are tired," he said.

"Not nearly as tired as you must be," I countered. "I wasn't in the thick of battle all day."

"You worry far too much about me," he complained, shoving his hand into the foliage and parting it so that we could see the water.

It was much closer than I expected. We must have come back from a different direction. He gestured for me to pass through, and on the other side, I realized we had arrived just above the place where the water met the pool below. The ground was slick with moss and wet rocks, but I recognized the path of stones that had taken us behind the falls the night before.

Slipping and stumbling, I worked my way down to the water. Behind me, I could hear him thrash and grunt as he nearly tumbled down the hill. I kept my face averted as he approached the water's edge. If I showed concern, I would insult him, and if I laughed…

He stepped out on the first stone, and held out his hand for me to follow.

Back inside the cave it felt cool and safe and held remarkable memories. After spending a day hot, and hungry, and terrified, the relief was so great I burst into tears.

He was lighting and hanging a lantern, but he turned to look at me. "Was it so bad that returning here makes you weep?" he asked, his mouth set in a grim line.

I shook my head, helplessly. I couldn't stop crying, no matter how much I wanted to, and I didn't know how to explain. "I-I'm sorry," I gulped. "I'm just…it was such a long…I'm sorry."

He reached across the chasm of emotion between us and touched my shoulder, briefly. "Sometimes the waiting and not knowing is worse than the being and knowing." He dropped to the ground and stretched, before folding his arms to make a pillow behind his head. "I am sorry I was so…" his eyes flicked away and he searched for a word, "cross. It was a very long day and I am very weary."

I wiped tears away with the edge of my shirt. "I understand." I knelt beside him and began to go through the pack he had brought along. Whatever food he had managed to grab as he left would have to serve as our meals for at least a day. I started an inventory.

"Dinah." There was something strange in his voice, a gentleness, an urgency.

I looked up at him. "Yes?"

He gestured. "Let me hold you for a while," he said. "I need the peace you bring me."

I eased myself against him, careful to avoid his wounded leg, and rested my head against his chest, smelling sweat and blood. "Like this?"

He stroked my hair. "I will miss this," he said, thoughtfully. "I should have never allowed myself to have it. All of my life I have denied myself the luxury of this…this restful intimacy, and this indulgence, now, so close to my-" he stopped as he felt my twinge of protest. "I will miss this," he repeated. "I will miss the belonging of you, the warmth, the compassion, this foolish independence of yours." His chest moved beneath my cheek as he laughed soundlessly.

"You could come with me," I suggested, toying with the idea as I toyed with the frayed ribbon of a medal on his shirt.

He stiffened and pulled his hand away from my hair. "No."

I rolled away from him. "I'll see about some food," I mumbled. I didn't want to think about what this conversation meant.

He rested while I put together some crackers and meat paste and some canned peaches. His breath was deep and labored. I couldn't help worrying about him. How could a man survive under the pressure that he had endured? Could his duty be this important to him?

He opened his eyes and caught me staring at him. "What is it?" he asked, lifting his head from the pillow of his arms. "Is something wrong?"

"No." I held out one of the battered tin plates I found in his kit, with the crackers and meat paste and peaches pooling in the dips and bumps. "I was just…" I took a deep breath. "What is this duty worth to you that you would suffer so much for the sake of it?"

He bit into a cracker and chewed, a corner of his mouth turned up, either in satisfaction or amusement. "*You* would ask me this?"

"I do." I took a bite of peach, dripping with syrup, and rubbed my chin self-consciously.

He looked at me for a moment before hitching himself up a little to point at me with the remains of the cracker. "What is your duty worth to you that you could come into a country on the verge of civil war, put your life and liberty in danger, live in the jungle with a man who could have taken you by force-" he ended the question by shoving the rest of the cracker into his mouth.

"But you didn't," I reminded him.

"No." He chewed and swallowed, and, pushing the tin plate away, fell back against the bedroll. "I did not."

I scooted forward a bit, wanting to see his face in the dim light of a single lantern. "Why?"

He frowned. "I do not know."

"Do you..." I struggled with the question, feeling my face getting hot with embarrassment. "Care for me – even a little?" Last night he had whispered that he loved me, both in English and in Spanish.

He seemed surprised by the question. He sat up again. "Did you leave any brandy after your attempt to drown me?"

That was not the response I was hoping for. Hurt, I scuttled around to the canteen, left on the floor near the backpack. "Yes, of course." I held it out to him.

He removed the cap, tilted the canteen and took one quick sip and then another. Putting the cap back in place he held it out to me. "I think I will sleep a while."

"Good idea." I waited until he was settled and went to the edge of the cave, to listen to the roar of the water and be bathed in the swirling mist. He had whispered 'I love you', I was certain of it. 'I will always love you,' he had said. 'I will go to my grave loving you.' I shivered at the memory. Last night we had been two lovers, beyond time, beyond politics. Last night there had been no war, no death, no terror, just two people loving and needing love. Why did there have to be a morning?

It was growing light again. I had given up my post at the water's edge and had come back to the bedroom, curling up near him but not touching him. At some point, he had turned and enveloped me in his arms. His lips were warm on my skin, and his hands became hot and demanding on my body. The lovemaking was swift, needy and silent. When it was over, we lay together, tangled in each other's arms, naked and peaceful.

Javier woke in the early morning, as the sun rose just enough to fill the space behind the water with an almost magical blue light. I rolled over, searching for him, and saw him standing at the water's edge, naked, hands on hips, looking like a Latin Adam, scowling at his war torn garden.

At my movement, he turned and the scowl softened. "Are you rested?"

I sat up, self-consciously drawing my knees up to shield my nakedness from his eyes. "I don't know how I could be," I said with a playful smile. "I seem to recall having my sleep disturbed last night. But, yes, I do feel rested."

"It is a great restorative, love-making," he agreed. His eyes slid over me. "And you are a most satisfying lover."

I ducked my head, shielding my blush from his eyes, as well. "Thank you."

He laughed at me, but it was a gentle, affectionate laugh. It didn't last, though. "We will need to leave soon, Dinah. Would you like a swim first? The water is cold, but it is bracing."

"Good. I need a bath." I pulled myself up, reaching for a shirt to cover myself.

He caught my hand as my fingers closed around the fabric. "Do not hide yourself from me, Dinah. I want to see you this way just once. I might never have another chance."

I looked away, quickly, before he saw the pain, and dropped the shirt, biting my lip to hold back a tearful protest.

"I brought this for you." He held out the white soap bar.

I am not a hard hearted person. I can be emotional, I can be sentimental...I *am* a sentimental person, but we had been warned before coming here that this reality was brutal and if we were to survive, we had to leave our feelings behind and act on facts and circumstances. That simple bar of soap was nearly the undoing of all my resolutions of stoicism, and pragmatism. I felt my voice tremble and my lip quiver under my teeth. "Thank you," I mumbled, taking it from his warm hand. With a gulp, I turned, running through the sheet of falling water, and down into the icy pool below, frantically attempting to escape my own brutal reality.

We walked miles that day, in heat, in dust, in silence. We went over open plains, crouching in high grass, pausing occasionally to listen to the unmistakable and unavoidable sounds of battle. Javier's heart was obviously there and not with me. I could see pain and guilt wash over his face every time we heard gunfire, or the screams of wounded men.

Finally, I gave up and settled down in the long, dry grass with a groan. "Just go back, Javier," I told him. "You can't think of anything else but what is going on over there," I pointed in the direction of the last round of gunfire. "I'm miserable enough without contributing to yours."

He turned around with a jerk. "Stand up, you foolish woman," he snapped, hauling me to my feet. "We must keep walking. We cannot afford to be overtaken."

"No." I pushed his hand way. "You want to be there, you are needed there and we both know it. Just give me a gun and point me in the right direction. It's okay, Javier. I understand duty and you have a duty to your men."

He wrapped an arm around me tightly and began pushing me forward. "When I found Roberto," he hissed, in short, painful bursts, "he was dying. He could not take enough breath to do more than whisper and every movement, every word was agony to him. I begged him to be still, but he would not."

"Javier, please," I implored.

He went on, ruthlessly. "He reminded me that I had vowed before God a new duty. I have vowed to take care of you." His grasp on me tightened slightly. "I must see you to the border, *mi jita*, or die trying." He released me. "Now, walk. It is *your* duty."

I stepped forward, stunned. Roberto ended his life on those words, for my sake? Javier cared enough about his old friend to heed his advice instead of going where he wanted to be? I turned to get his attention, and realized when he jerked his face away, that there was a tear cutting a trail through the dust on his face. I turned forward and walked.

By dusk we had found shelter in the low lying ridge of a rock jutting out from the first rise of the foothill. Javier went in first to make certain there were no rebels or snakes, and then he gestured for me to follow. We ate the rest of the crackers and meat paste hunched over in the cave, and when the night had devoured the last rays of the sun, we made love in the thick silence, and fell asleep locked in each other's arms.

We didn't make it to the border the next day. When we woke the next morning, the battle had moved around us, cutting us off. So we went east, toward the coast. And the next morning, so had the fighting. We alternated between running and hiding, scrounging for anything edible. Sometimes we found trees still harboring fruit, sometimes we resorted to grass and water. I learned a harsh lesson in those days, learning the true definition of want, and what I would be willing to eat if I got hungry enough.

At night, we just wanted shelter. Sometimes we found a cave, or a well hidden clearing. Once we slept in a ditch beside a road, covered in grass, and as we lay there, trying not to make a sound or cause the grass to move, we listened to rebels moving past, guns clattering, as they whispered and planned.

The days became a weary pattern of this before we woke up one morning to find ourselves behind the lines of battle, and fell in with the scattered remnant of Javier's own troops. They had been driven far North by the fierce determination of the rebellious peasants and the brutality of government supplied weapons.

Resentment ran high among those who had survived the slaughter. They blamed Javier for ignoring the whispers of outside intervention, they blamed him for not organizing any sort of withdrawal plan, for now they suffered from lack of food, ammunition and medical supplies. But, most of all they blamed him for losing his head to, as I heard one of them describe me, *un manojo de pelo blanco plateado y ojos azules* - a bundle of silver white hair and blue eyes. Under other circumstances, I might be flattered, but now I was just embarrassed for Javier's sake.

Javier did not offer any explanations or apologies for his behavior. He just moved into the ragged encampment, assessed it and began giving orders. The orders were followed, albeit resentfully. An infirmary, of sorts, was established and despite orders to the opposite, I was compelled to try and give aid and comfort wherever I could.

Javier found me as evening fell, our third day in camp. I was bathing sweat from the brow of a dying soldier, and trying not to cry as he wept for his mother.

"Dinah, what are you doing here?"

I wrung the rag into a chipped metal basin. "Trying to break a fever," I answered evenly. There was no need to advertise that it was an exercise in futility. The man was in enough distress, why tell him there was no hope?

"That is from a mosquito bite, Dinah." He jerked me up from my kneeling position. "Do you know what that means?"

"Yes," I said quietly, darting a glance at the soldier. "Malaria. And I've taken all the medication and preparations. I can't just let him lie there and suffer."

"Dinah," he growled, marching me away from the area, "why do you torment this way? I made a vow to get you to the border. I will not have crossed miles of treacherous country for you to die because of a careless disrespect for disease. You may be a nurse, but you are not immortal." He shook her roughly. "I told you to stay away from there, I will not see you there again. Do you understand?"

I nodded, shaking loose of his grasp. "But, please, can't you do something about the flies? Some of the wounds have festered and I saw-"

"Dinah." His voice was anguished. "Go back to where you were sitting and wait for me."

"But-"

"Go." When I remained still, stubbornly refusing to be ordered around or to abandon my duty, he sighed. "I will try. I give my word."

I surrendered my position, relieved, at least, for the wounded. The conditions in that so called infirmary had been enough to send me out that morning, desperately ill. My inability to look at such devastating affliction by one man to another caused to me to doubt my vocation. Maybe I ought to consider teaching, I thought, rubbing my back with chapped, stiff fingers. Maybe I ought to settle down, get married and raise children – I looked up so swiftly that the green cap fell into my eyes. Dinah, you *are* married. Could you ever settle for any other man after loving Javier Contreras?

I felt the tears well in my eyes as I searched the campsite. I saw him, tall, square-shouldered, strong hands gesturing toward the infirmary area, his dark face crinkled up as he squinted into the sun. "And I do love you, Javier," I whispered. "I'll go to my grave loving you."

Javier brought a tin plate of frijoles to me as night fell. "Eat, *mi jita*. These last few days are showing on you." He put the plate before me. "You are getting thin."

I picked up the spoon and scowled at the tannish gray lump before me. Looking back, I suppose I should have fallen on that food like a ravenous dog, but I wasn't sure I could have swallowed a bite of it.

Javier settled beside me, his own plate in hand. He laughed, a short burst of wry observation. "Not quite the same as the first meal we shared together."

I thought back to the opulent surroundings, the rich good, the lead cut crystal from which he poured Napoleon brandy, the overpowering hate I had felt for him. “No,” I agreed, taking an un-enthusiastic bite, “not at all.”

He watched me struggle with the un-appetizing fare. For a moment, I thought saw some hint of the heart within the man, some shade of compassion, but it folded back within the black fire of his eyes and he shifted, and spoke rather off-handed. “You are bearing up impressively. You have earned a reluctant respect from these men.”

“Thank you.” Hunger overtook aesthetics and I began to eat quickly. “Although, I can’t say that I’ll ever enjoy camping again.”

He laughed again, but sobered instantly. “This is not camping, Dinah.” He gestured around us. “This is survival.”

I pushed the plate away. “And I’m surviving as best as I can.”

He reached out a finger to trace a dark half-moon under my eye. “You are tired, Dinah. I am not letting you get enough rest.”

“I don’t mind,” I blurted out, and then blushed furiously.

His smile was thoughtful. “You have much love in you, Dinah. I envy the man who takes you when I am gone.”

“Oh, Javier,” I sighed, “I don’t want-”

"Shh." He moved closer and kissed me. "It will happen, Dinah. We cannot ignore what is going on here. The end is near." His hands slid around me and held tight. "I am grateful to God that He allowed me days and nights with you to remember in purgatory. Do not give me guilt to savor, with your vows of faithfulness to a heart that no longer beats, no longer loves." His voice was tortured, his face pinched and his fingers seemed to bury themselves in the flesh of my arms.

I swallowed my profession of love and let him hold me against his chest. My purgatory would begin the day we parted – no, that would be the day my life became Hell.

Javier turned my face to his and gently brushed a tear away. "You should not cry, querida," he scolded gently. "The time to cry was the day you came into my possession, for that was the day that your future was sealed." He looked down at the tear still resting on his fingertip, and he nearly smiled. "No protest, woman?"

"No," I sniffed. "It's true."

The smile grew sly. "Oh, then you admit you are a possession?"

I sat up. "Are you trying to start a fight, Javier?" I deliberately mispronounced his name.

I saw anger blaze in his eyes for a second and then the smile returned. "You draw a sword as sharp as mine, do you not, *mi jita?*" He flicked the tear away and tangled his fingers in my hair. "My name is easy to remember if you think of having – as I have you."

I glanced away, noticing that darkness was almost total, now, as all fires had been extinguished lest they gave away our position. It reminded me that there was so little time left. I didn't want to waste any of it jockeying for a position that was practically meaningless. I buried my face in the opening of his shirt, letting my lips brush a mat of coiled black hair and salty skin. "Whatever you say," I murmured.

Neither of us knew then it was our last night together. The morning came, the battle began, and nothing mattered but surviving for another day.

We were driven further north that afternoon. It was horrible. It was not men killing men, it wasn't even a battle. Somehow, Javier learned that the government fueled rebel machine was surging toward us, and he gave orders to retreat.

His troops were stunned by his reaction. They wanted to take their stand there, and fight until the last man had fallen. They accused Javier of cowardice, insanity, betrayal. They said he was surrendering the cause for the life of a woman. I was devastated, but Javier withstood it all, arguing that they had already sustained too many losses, they were low on food and ammunition. To stay and fight meant certain death, to withdraw and regain strength would allow them the chance to find – and win – another day. His reasons eventually prevailed and then began the most horrible aspect.

Javier had learned that the rebels now had tanks, which changed the whole complexion of the battle. Insisting that we were fighting time, he ordered the men to break camp and move deeper into the hills. As there was only one functioning Jeep in camp, only essential supplies were to be taken, and anything men wanted to carry, they'd have to take it out on their own back, and on their own feet.

It took me a moment to realize that he meant us to abandon every injured soldier who was not capable of walking. I might have gone mad at that point, racing across the chaotic compound, screaming Javier's name. He was inventorying the last of the food and ammunitions as they were loaded into the Jeep. "How could you?" I cried, slapping at him. "You heartless son of a-"

"Dinah." He caught me around my waist, pulling me against him so that I could neither hit him nor run away. He sounded more annoyed than anything, speaking to me as if I were no more than a pupping nipping his heels. "Not now, I'm busy." He set me down a few feet from the Jeep. "Get your things together." He resumed his inspection.

I couldn't look at him. All I could see was a dozen or more men in varying degrees of pain and helplessness left lying on cots under a blistering sun. "You're a murderer," I spat.

"Be silent,"" he commanded, coldly.

"They're all going to die," I protested, in tears, swinging my fists at him. "I hate you."

"I said enough," he roared and slapped me with the back of his hand hard enough to send me sprawling backward in the dirt.

I lay there for a moment, stunned, wiping blood from my mouth. Javier held tableau for a moment, looking down at me in confusion, anger and pain, before he turned back to the Jeep again.

Two of the soldiers who had been loading the Jeep shifted toward me, uncertainly, and reached down to lift me from the ground. I shrugged them off and marched away, furious. I would never forgive him for what he was doing. Never.

Our conflict had started a controversy in the encampment. My Spanish was sufficient to understand that there were two distinct positions on the matter. Some men believed that *La Senora* was only trying to save lives and cared about the soldiers more than the *Capitan*, and he was too heartless to listen to her. Others believed that I was only interfering and that the *Capitan* had tolerated far too much from me already, and it was far past the time when he should put me in my place.

No one asked my opinion on the matter. No one even looked at me. I sat on a rock out of the way, trying not to cry for those men silenced by injury or imminent death. "I hate this place," I muttered around a swollen lip. "I hate the flies and the dirt and the heat and the beans for every meal and the foul tasting water and the lewd looks from the soldiers and never being able to take a real bath or sleep in a real bed, and most of all, I hate Javier!" What I really hated most was that I didn't hate him, and if he were to come across that compound and even look at me kindly, I'd probably fly into his arms and forgive everything he had ever done or might ever do.

When he did finally come toward me, an hour later, I was sitting back against the rock, my arms wrapped around my knees, shivering and feeling just a little faint from dehydration. He approached me almost tentatively, waiting for some remark or reaction from me. He got none.

He looked down at me, hands on hips, focusing on my lip, which was now swollen and probably bright purple. He frowned at me, his tongue touching his own lip, as if testing the pain of such an injury. There was a strange mix of emotions evident in his face. "Are you through with your righteous," he paused to find the word, "indignation?"

I glanced away as if I hadn't heard him. It was childish, I know, but I wasn't through with my righteous indignation. No, not at all.

"These are my men," he continued, beginning to pace in front of me. "I shall make decisions as I see fit." He smacked his fist into his opened palm. "I have more to think of than my own conscience," he continued, and the authoritative tone seemed to waver. He looked down at me, waiting for a response.

I continued to look elsewhere.

"It is not an easy thing to be in command," he said, as if patiently explaining the situation to someone too stupid to understand. "Especially in such terrible times. To be responsible for so many lives..." he shrugged. "And to complicate matters with the presence of an American woman, whose safety the entire world demands, makes this possible...impossible." His voice hardened. "It takes a strong man to hold this position. And I am strong enough." Again, his tongue went gingerly to the corner of his mouth.

I'd had firsthand knowledge of his strength. At that moment, I was not impressed.

He watched me for a moment, waiting. At last he sighed. "Perhaps I am not strong enough." He turned and walked several steps away before whirling around. "Are you not going to say anything?" he snapped, as if challenging me to complain.

I still did not look at him. I don't think I even blinked.

Javier moved within an arm's reach of me. He swallowed and began an awkward speech, in a very hushed voice. "I am sorry, Dinah, that I struck you – but, you deserved it." His voice lifted as his face darkened in anger. "You cannot speak to me that way," he finished haughtily.

I felt heat rising in my cheeks but I did not respond, I did not even flinch as he spoke.

He paced around me for a moment before speaking again. His voice was again muted, but irritated. "Will you not at least accept my apology?"

I arched a brow in surprise. I hadn't heard an apology, I hadn't heard any regret for his actions, only absurd justifications.

"You are an insolent, insubordinate creature," he pronounced, backing away from me. "If you were one of my soldiers, I would have you shot."

I let the upraised brow drop, slowly. Inside, I was stunned – horrified – but he mustn't see that.

He swore hotly and marched away, into the darkness.

I shivered, and slumped against the rock.

Chapter Eight
The Choice

Almost instantly, he returned, falling on his knees in front of me. His hands gripped my wrists, roughly. For a moment, I feared he had arranged an impromptu firing squad for me and intended to drag me to my doom. Instead, he merely shook me and pleaded, "Please, Dinah, say you will forgive me. I did not want to hurt you, but I had to assert my authority, for your sake. If these men see me as weak now, not only will my life be worthless, but you would be in immediate danger, without my protection." He buried his head in my arms. "For the love of God, Dinah, speak to me."

"How could you leave them behind?" I asked. "It's murder, Javier."

"No, Dinah," he jerked back from me, rocking onto his heels, "it is war. To take that handful of men who will die, anyway, would assure the death of every other one among us." He sighed, and dragged his hair back from his eyes, wearily. "I know it seemed to be a cruel decision, but I had to make it."

"We would never make such a decision where I come from," I told him, coldly.

"You do not know that," he answered. "There has not been war on your soil in over one hundred years. But, I ask you this," he raised a finger to emphasize his point, "how many captains have gone down with their ship? How many men have sacrificed for the lives of women and children? Why do your men even go to war, but to protect the innocents at home?"

"But this captain isn't going down with his ship," I protested. "This captain is running off into the hills."

"If I do not go, they do not go." He shrugged. "Perhaps it would have been better in your eyes for us all to wait, like pigs in a pen, for slaughter?" When I did not answer, because I honestly did not have an answer, he shrugged again. "I know you can never reconcile yourself to this decision, Dinah, but you must listen to me. It is necessary for the rest to survive."

"If they don't go, I don't go," I said, my chin jutting out defiantly.

"What?" he rasped. "You cannot stay. There are men with machine guns and tanks marching down on us at this moment."

"The camp is filled with such men right now," I shot back. "And I am staying. I'm a nurse, Javier. I can't leave them behind."

He shook an authoritarian fist at me. "I am taking you to the border, *mujer*, as agreed. You will not argue with me."

I'm not arguing," I snapped. "I'm just not going."

Javier sighed in exasperation. "I did not rescue you from my own men, I did not smuggle you out of a den of ravaging wolves, I did not order the death of a man who put his hands on you, I did not…give…you…my…name, only to leave you behind to be killed by the rebels you came here to aide. I will not leave you here."

"You could stay, too," I suggested.

"I have sworn to get you to the border," he repeated.

"Or die trying," I retorted.

"But not to kill you," he shouted. "You *will* go with me, Dinah."

"No."

"Dinah." There was a mix of torment and anger in his rough voice. "You will not force me to use my authority again, *por favor*."

"What will you do?" I challenged, infuriated by his threat. "Hit me again? Drag me out by my hair?"

"No." He knelt beside me. "I will tie you up and carry you out on my shoulders," he promised, "like a wounded deer."

"You wouldn't"!"

He caught my wrists, wrenched them behind me, and stood, forcing me to my feet. "Do you doubt that I could?"

"No." I twisted, painfully, in his grasp. "Let me go."

He released me, and backed away several steps. "You will go, Dinah."

"Bully," I hissed, rubbing my wrists. How could I ever be attracted to such an animal? How could I ever give my heart or my body to him?

"Dinah." His voice grew just slightly less harsh. "In your heart you know I am right. Stop hating me for a decision I have no choice in making."

I sighed. Was I really so transparent? "I don't hate you, Javier. I just don't understand you."

"There is nothing to understand but that I know my duty." He turned away as if to leave, but stopped and looked over his shoulder at me. "Do not ever force me to demonstrate my authority again. I felt as if I had hit myself." He turned around and I was surprised to see pain in his expression which could match my own. "But, you must under-stand, I had to do it. My authority is precarious enough. I cannot have a mere woman refute it."

"I did not realize I was a 'mere woman'," I murmured, still rubbing at my chafed and twisted arms. "I thought I was your wife."

"Which gives you even less right to question or disobey me, here," he answered. "This is not the

United States. You do not have the same…" he searched for a word, "position, here."

I forced my hands into the pockets of my shorts before he could see that they had curled into fists. "So I see." I let my tongue trace over the area swelling up in the wake of his slap. "Don't worry, Javier. I'll never get close enough to you to let you hit me again."

I heard him make a sound – exasperated disappointment would be the best way to describe it, and he moved a little closer. "You will not stay away from me, *mi esposa*," he said in a low purr. "Our time is running out and we will take every advantage that we can."

Something cold raced through me, tamping down the fire of my anger. "What is going to happen?" I whispered.

He reached for my arms and pulled my hands free from my pockets. "That I do not know." He pressed my hands to his chest.

"You do know," I protested, but I didn't try to break free. "Roberto knew. He told me."

"Roberto was a sentimental fool," he declared. "Kindhearted but a fool all the same. He talked too much."

My fingers curled into the fabric of his shirt. "Tell me the truth, Javier. You owe it to me, I am your wife."

"And for that reason I should reveal military intelligence?"

"Yes," I insisted. "I am a part of you. I have the right to know if I am going where you go." I nodded toward the camp. "I want to know what's out there waiting for us."

He looked back to the camp, as well. "Did Roberto tell you he once held a very high office in the old government?"

I shook my head.

"I am talking many, many years ago. My father disappeared under that regime and Roberto and some of his men came to the mission where my father had left me." He struggled with a memory. "They were supposed to find any of his family or collaborators and all they found was me."

I gasped.

He shrugged. "He could have had me killed, but he did not. He would not make a good soldier."

"He had compassion, Javier," I chided, hoping he couldn't hear the pain in my voice. "Sometimes that is an advantage."

"It is true, he was caring, and sympathetic. He came into the mission with a gun in his hand, just like all the others, but even I could see he could not justify shooting an eleven year old boy just because my father might have said a word or two of his plans in my hearing.

"He put me in the confessional and told me not to make a sound. Then he sent all the other men to look in the stables, and told me he would come back for me and he did, later that night. He risked his life for me. He taught me the weaknesses and strengths of our government, and where my father was right and where he was wrong. He made me what I am." There was a quiver of loss in his voice and he worked his jaw against the rage and pain that demanded to be expressed. "He would have been shot as a traitor for saving me."

"Doesn't that tell you anything, Javier?" I asked.

"What?" He brushed my words away impatiently. "What do you babble about?"

"Your cause is wrong, too, Javier," I insisted, reaching out for him before he walked away. "The military is no better than the old government; it, too, is power hungry. You've done nothing for these people except add to their poverty and misery. The only people who have prospered from your rule was the military itself."

"Be quiet," he growled.

"You were wrong, Javier." He took a step away and I followed. "Are you really so blind? Admit it, the people-"

"I said be quiet!" he roared and his hand swung back as if to strike me again.

I waited. I did not cower. I knew his power, I knew his strength, I knew the pain he was capable of inflicting, but I wasn't going to surrender now, not when he was so close to understanding his mistakes. After all, it was still my right to say what I believe and threats would not rob me of that right.

He met my eyes and saw that I was not going to back down, no matter what he threatened to do. He lowered his hand, slowly. "Be packed," he barked. "We are leaving as soon as it is dark."

We traveled for days – or rather, nights, sleeping where we could find shelter in daylight, and moving slowly and cautiously under cover of darkness. I lost track of time. I was tired, I was hungry and I was angry. Every step, every sound reminded me of the cruel act we had committed in the name of safety.

Javier did not attempt to console or mollify me. He marched ahead of me most nights, and slept near me – when he slept – only for appearance' sake. We didn't speak. We rarely made eye contact. I hated him, and yet...

The heat was almost unbearable. Our water supply was gone and many men had taken to drinking from stagnant pools. I managed to resist that temptation, but the subsequent dehydration left me achy, nauseated, and slightly delirious. I couldn't sleep during the day, and all I could do at night was march behind Javier, putting one foot in front of the other.

Finally, we encountered a river, and men dived in, heedless of any potential dangers. I nearly did as well, but Javier held me back, went to the water's edge and brought back a canteen filled with water. "Crocodiles," he said, tersely.

I emptied the canteen so quickly my head swam. I wanted to fill it again, just to let the cool water wash over me, but Javier ignored my request. "This is where we leave them," he told me, bringing back both our canteens. We will go north, along this river. The border is perhaps two days walk from here."

"And them?" I asked, wiping my mouth.

"Another command," he nodded toward the river, "on the other side. They will join up there."

"And you?" I asked, belatedly, as he shouldered our bags.

He shrugged. "We will see."

His evasive answer bothered as much as his aloof behavior. I got up and followed, reluctantly. The sun was already starting to glimmer over the hills east of us, and I wondered how long we would march before finding a place to hide and rest. I slapped at a mosquito and pulled the bill of his cap forward on my brow to keep the sunlight from my burning eyes. Javier never even looked back. I could have fallen in my tracks and he wouldn't even know.

Finally, he found a young banana tree, where the broad leaves formed a nest low to the ground. He spread the leaves apart and indicated that I could sit there and rest. I sank to the ground with a grateful groan.

He stood above me, frowning. "You have been very slow the last few days." He looked up to the brilliant, yellow sky. "We are not making many miles today."

"I know," I agreed painfully, rolling over to rest my cheek on my bedroll.

"How is your stomach?" he asked politely.

"Empty," I asked, flatly, "and I'm glad."

He settled down in front of me, looking out toward the path we had made in the foliage. "And your back?"

"Still very sore." I straightened my legs and stretched tentatively. Our conversation was hardly the intimate chatter of lovers, but at least it was communication. I watched him pull the gun from his holster and turn it over in his hands. "How much further?"

He slid his gun back into the holster. "At this rate? Two days, perhaps three. I had hoped to be there today." He reached for his canteen. "We went too far out of our way finding a safe place for the others to cross, and all we have managed since is to come back to the place where we left camp." He tipped his head in the direction we had been walking.

"Then they might be-"

"Dinah, it has been sixteen days since we left them. If they have not starved to death or succumbed to their wounds, the rebels have surely finished them off." His voice was detached, as if he thought showing no emotion would be more kind.

"Oh." I settled back against the bedroll, heavily. "I'm beginning to wish you'd left me there in the village to my own resources."

"You're not giving up now, are you?" He seemed astounded. "I have believed all along that you would be marching after I fell in my tracks."

I suppose he thought he was being affectionate, but I couldn't muster a smile. "I'm not a soldier, Javier," I answered wearily. "I never was."

He shook his head, his eyes focused above mine. "You have been a better soldier than I have ever before commanded." Out of nowhere came a wry chuckle. "Yet, you do not know how to take commands." The laughter faded, but his eyes never met mine.

"Not true." I shifted uncomfortably. "I only follow the important ones."

Javier was studying the foliage behind me. "Is this true?"

I nodded sleepily.

"Then," he said very quietly, "I command you to get up."

I wanted to argue, but something in his expression, in his hushed voice told me not to question. I rolled to my knees and then to my feet.

He hunched himself over one knee, his body blocking the action of his hands. He was tugging that little gun from my bag. "Dinah," he said so quietly I had to watch his mouth to be sure he was speaking. "Take this and start walking." He gestured with the gun. "That way. Quickly." He stood and, taking my shoulders, turned me in the proper direction. "Go," he hissed in my ear, "and do not stop, do not turn around. This is a very important command."

I obeyed. He had seen something and I didn't know what it was, but I knew better than to question him now. I started walking away from the banana tree, in the direction we had just come. I had gone fifty or sixty paces before I heard the shouting. Don't look back, I told myself as I broke into a run. Javier can handle himself. He'll finish them off and then catch up to me. I repeated this in a whisper, matching the rhythm of my pounding steps, but I seemed to run for an eternity without him and, at last, I faltered, and then stopped.

Counting to ten to prepare myself, I turned slowly. Javier was not behind me. There was not even enough of a breeze to rustle the leaves and give me hope. I took a step or two in the direction I had come, despite Javier's warning still ringing in my ears. Then another, and another, and then I was running back the way I had come.

I stopped just where my own broken path began to turn toward the banana trees. On the ground near where we had been sitting two men lay, bleeding, dead, their eyes wide and unseeing, and I tore my gaze from them in horror, feeling my stomach spin, feeling my blood chill. Beyond them, two men rolled on the ground in mortal combat. I stared, I willed – I prayed victory for Javier. I knew he was weak and tired, as hungry and physically depleted as I, but I wanted to believe he was superhuman enough to win the contest.

The other man managed to gain the upper position, his hands against Javier's throat, pushing and squeezing. Javier, beneath him, kicked as if trying to gain purchase in the dusty ground, and suddenly his attacker stiffened, back arched, cried out and rolled to his side. Coughing and gasping, Javier made it to one knee, blood dripping from his mouth, seeping through his shirt.

I was about to step forward and call his name when I saw, behind him, with incredible stealth, a fourth man crept forward, a long, silver knife in his hand. I didn't have the wits or the time to cry out; I found the gun in my hand and raised it. I pulled the trigger. I saw a mist of red before my eyes. I fainted.

"Dinah, can you hear me?" The words were gentle, warm, worried. "Dinah, wake up. It is over."

I opened my eyes slowly, not certain what I would see. Javier was kneeling over me, the little silver gun in his hand. "Javier," I cried, sitting up, clutching his arm. "That-that man-"

"Shh." He eased me backward to the ground. "It is over, *mi jita*, do not think about it."

"But, he was going to-"

"I know, I know." An unexpected and incongruous grin flashed across his grimy, bloody face. "I am so very glad you cannot take orders, after all."

I tried to smile, too, but couldn't. "I sh-shot him, didn't I?"

"*Si*." The smile vanished. "If you had not, he would have killed me." He tucked the gun out of sight. "Can you walk?"

I didn't think I could; I felt like jelly, but I knew I couldn't just lie there and think things over. "Yes, I want to get away from here!"

He helped me to my feet, carefully shielding my view of the bloody aftermath. "I thought I heard something as we were talking," he said, his arm wrapped around my waist and forcing me forward. "I knew I could not get us both far enough away in time, but I would not allow you to sit and waiting for an ambush with me." He staggered a little, pressed his free hand to his side, and forced himself upright again. "I did not expect to survive that."

"That's why you told me not to come back," I finished, beginning to find my own strength again. "I'm glad I did, anyway."

He collected the packs and bedroll, and put his arm around me again, walking more quickly, but lurching awkwardly forward. "We must not stop again until nightfall. Now that they know where we are, it's very likely they will do everything they can to prevent us getting to the border."

"Can we get there?"

"We will try."

We walked, limped and dragged ourselves forward in silence. It was obvious that Javier had sustained yet another wound, but he wouldn't stop to let me examine him. When the sun had finally ceased its merciless torture, it was dark and cool almost immediately. At least, that's how it felt to me.

Javier dropped the bedrolls on the path. "We will stay right here tonight," he said. "It is a natural path. The animals will come, but we will just have to run that risk." He pulled the gun from its holster and gestured with it. "The animals we might be able to fight, but the snakes in there, we might not."

"Snakes?" I inched closer to him.

"*Si.*" He dropped down on the bedroll.

"Oh, this is too much." I sank to my own bedroll, tears welling up in my eyes, despair welling up in my soul. "I give up, Javier. I can't take it anymore."

He leaned forward enough to put a bloodied hand on my shoulder. It should have registered with me that he was still bleeding from somewhere on his torso, but all I could think about was my own misery. "Shh," he murmured, "easy, *mi jita*. It will be over soon."

"It's just too much, Javier," I wept.

"You have had the worst of days," he admitted, quietly. "You have been sick, you have not had sleep or food, you have had a frightening en..." he scowled into the blackness, looking for the word. "Encounter. You, who have dedicated your life to saving others, will never reconcile yourself to having taken a life. You have every right to feel as if you cannot go on. But, you will. I know this." He brushed my tangled hair back from my tear wet face. "I know this about you, Dinah de Contreras. You are not a – a quitter. You will pick yourself up and survive. I have seen you do it before and I will see you do it this time."

"You seem so kind and understanding," I sniffed, trying to sit up straight again. "How did you ever get to be so mean and rotten?"

He laughed and eased down against the bedroll. "It is the way of life," he said. "The way dirty children starve in the streets and men wearing grand uniforms eat like kings that they believe they are."

I looked back at him, astonished. "Javier, do you realize what you just said?"

I could see him repeat the words to himself, consider their significance and discard it. "I did not mean me, *mujer*," he corrected with effort. "I was thinking of places I studied in school. I had a tender heart for people in need…then."

"Then," I repeated with emphasis. "Today you could turn your back on a starving child."

"Today?" He chuckled roughly. "Today we are the starving children, no?"

"Some would call it karma," I answered bitterly.

"Perhaps." His voice was more a heavy sigh than a sound.

I turned sharply at it. "Javier, just how badly did they hurt you?" I fumbled to get nearer.

He waved me away. "Do not concern yourself. It is not…" he pressed his hand to his side as if in pain, "your karma."

"Javier!" I forced his hand away and lifted his shirt. He was still bleeding, hours after the injury, though had coagulated thickly around the wound, making it impossible for me to determine if it had come from a knife or a gun. "What hap-pened?" I fumbled the backpack, hoping I had even a little antiseptic left. There was none, but I did find, at the bottom of my bag, a small bottle of mouth-wash. I unscrewed the cap and spilled some over the wound.

He reacted with a gasp and a stream of Spanish that I'm sure he would never repeat in the Church.

Using the corner of my shirt, I daubed at the wound. "Good," I said grimly. "If you can swear at me like that, you're still too mean to die." I pulled a tee shirt from the bag and pressed it against his side. "Hold still. Dear God, Javier, why didn't you say something. You could have died."

He shrugged.

"You bastard! What would happen to me if you dropped dead out here in the…in the…" It was no use. The tears began again.

"I'm sorry." His hand sought me, and landed on my arm. "I'm very sorry. I should have put you on that train myself."

"Oh, save your breath," I snapped, wiping his blood from my hands. "The train was leaving when I got there."

"I…I could have stopped it further up the tracks," he said, struggling for breath, "but it didn't seem so important then."

"Javier," I said more sternly, "stop talking."

"I wanted you for a day or two," he persisted. "How would have thought this rebellion would have gone on so long."

"That shows how little you know about the spirit and strength of people who crave freedom," I said.

He ignored my challenge, his eyes closed, his breathing more regular, his hand reaching for mine once again. "Perhaps I do not understand them, but in honesty, did you believe such disorganized, ignorant people with nothing but a belief to guide them could last seven weeks – even with guns and supplies from the old regime?"

"I'm surprised they listened to the promises of the old – seven weeks?" I looked back at him. "That's not possible."

"Then perhaps *you* do not know these people as well as-"

"Seven weeks?" I repeated, drawing up on my knees, almost ready to run for my life. "Are you sure it has been seven weeks?"

He worked himself up on an elbow. "I am sure. Does it seem so long?"

"It seems like an eternity," I confessed, trying to put the last few weeks of my life into a mental timeline. "And yet, somehow, it seems as if it's only been a day."

"You have done much living in seven weeks," he conceded, tugging distractedly at the leather strap of my rucksack. "But, *si*, it has already been seven weeks since the day we...met. In fact," he rubbed his eyes, "tomorrow would be *nuestro aniversario* – a suitable day to part, no?" He chuckled.

"Anniversary?" I asked. "Of what?"

He reached up and tugged at the bill of the cap until it tumbled into my lap. "Six weeks ago we married." He smiled. I could see his teeth flashing white in the moonlight. "What American husband would remember such a thing?"

"Six weeks," I repeated, still dazed. It couldn't be possible. How could I have survived so long? He must be wrong. I wished, pointlessly for my appointment book, left behind in the clinic when we packed to leave, a lifetime ago. I could no longer remember the day of the week. Was it January? Could it be February? "What month is it?"

"It is the beginning of March," he answered, falling back to the bedroll. "It is not good that I remembered?"

"March? What happened to February?"

"We marched through it." He yawned and opened his eyes again. "It is not good?"

"Yes, yes," I muttered. How could I have missed an entire month? Impossible, I told myself again. I haven't even – I straightened in shock, fear mingling with hope. Could I be pregnant?

"Dinah?" Javier shifted upward and touched my arm. "Are you ill? Your face is very pale."

I blinked away tears before I looked in the direction of his anxious face. "Oh, no, fine. Surprised, that's all." He didn't look convinced so I added an emphatic, "Really."

Should I tell him? "I-" No, not yet. He had too much on his mind already, and he had been injured. I saw no reason to add more to his worries, especially in his weakened state. And what if…the tears threatened again, and I looked away. What if he did not want responsibility? He had expressed an interest in having children, but there was no reason to suppose that he would want a child with me. What if he resented my child the way he resented the child of that poor woman? The idea made my stomach roll threateningly. "Really." I repeated.

He eased back against the bedroll, still looking at me, unconvinced. He would want to be responsible, I decided. He would want to care for it, to give it his name. Perhaps if he knew, he might agree to come back to the U.S. with me, for the sake of his-our child.

I'm not even sure there is a child. It could be a dozen other things: fatigue, stress, fear, some kind of stomach ailment from unclean water or poor food. I had been very careful, but I couldn't be sure I'd avoided all the pitfalls of a bad water supply. Emotions can wreak havoc on a woman's cycle.

Then again, I have experienced all the typical symptoms, I argued, poor sleep, morning sickness, and I've been unusually sensitive.

Then again, it could just be the water.

But, it could be…it could be. I swallowed back the hope so it wouldn't be evident in my eyes or my voice. "I'm fine," I repeated.

His eyes registered his doubt. "You looked so sad just now," he said, shifting restlessly, "as if you had thought of the most terrible thing in the world." He reached out, slide his knuckle against my cheek. "After the last seven weeks, what could only now appear so terrible that you would look that way?"

Sad? Was it the saddest thing in the world? No, the saddest thing was wanting to enjoy his touch, encourage it, take it further, even in the middle of a stew of dangers I had only just begun to comprehend. But, was a child conceived in this stew, with a man who might not live another month, a man whose politics and morals were diametrically opposed to mine, a man who was cruel and domineering, a man in whose arms I wanted to spend the rest of my life the saddest thing I could imagine? "Oh, no," I denied, sighing. It wasn't sad, sad at all. "I'm tired, that's all. As you said, this has been a very difficult day."

I'm not sure he was convinced, but he didn't probe further. He lay back and opened his arms, inviting me into his embrace. "Then you should sleep."

Sleep? I knew I wouldn't sleep. My mind was already whirling ahead, learning to knit booties and sing lullabies, choosing names. I would name him Javier – or perhaps Janice after my mother, or-

"Go to sleep, Dinah," he admonished, gently. "There is nothing here to harm you. You are safe. You can sleep and be safe, knowing I will protect you."

"Yes, Sir," I said, meekly.

"Bueno. You will feel better after some sleep." He rubbed my arm, not gently, though I think he meant it to be affectionate. "Sleep will cure everything."

"Yes, Doctor."

His hand stilled on my arm. "An English lesson, please. Does 'playing doctor' mean what I believe it means?"

I sat up and was surprised to see an almost naughty smile on his weary face. "Where did you hear an expression like that?"

He gestured faintly. "One of your compatriots. It was some time before I met you. I happened upon a conversation in the cantina, and heard an American speaking of a woman he lusted after – I suspect it was you, because he described your yellow-white hair. He said he would like to play doctor with that nurse." The humor in his face and the ease of his posture vanished. "If I had known you then, I might have shot him."

"Then I'm glad you didn't know me then." I looked away from him. "You have to stop shooting people for looking at me."

"No matter. It seems unlikely to happen again." He was quiet for a moment, as if he was looking into the future. "Does it mean make love to?"

I looked at him. "Not exactly." How strange that I'm not even curious which doctor had said that about me. "It does imply sexual play."

His face crumpled a bit, as if tasting something bitter. "I do not believe that playing with you was his goal."

I was at a loss. "Well, it's really something children do." When I saw his horrified expression, I rushed on. "You know, experimenting, discovering the differences between boys and girls. Didn't you ever try to see the differences when you were a little boy?"

"No," he said emphatically. "Did you-"

"No!"

"Then I do not understand where the saying came from."

"Oh, let's not discuss it anymore," I said irritably. "It's too embarrassing."

"It should not be embarrassing to discuss anything with one's husband, *mujer*," he chided. "I did not mean to sound…old fashioned, I just do not like to think of any man – regardless of his age – looking at you the way I've seen you."

"Well, I doubt it is something you need to worry about." I wanted the conversation to stop. I wanted him to rest. I wanted to go back to my plans and daydreams. I settled against him, hoping he would let the topic drift away.

I could feel him chuckle beneath me. "That is not to say that I would not like to play doctor with you at any time."

That newly discovered warmth of anticipation slid over me, becoming a central and powerful heat somewhere in my middle. "Nor I." Feeling as if some-thing more were expected of me, I reached behind me to caress his thigh.

To my surprise, he moved my hand gently, but determinedly, away. "Not tonight, *mi jita*. This day has been too long and too bloody. All I want from you tonight is rest." He pulled his jacket over to cover us both. "*Buenos noches, Senora* Contreres."

"Good night, Mr. Contreres," I answered. He can be nurturing, I reflected, looking up at the black sky. . He could be a wonderful father, if he allowed himself – especially with a son. In the dark canvas above us, I could almost see him with a miniature version of himself riding on his shoulders, laughing and shrieking in delight. I could see his eyes glow with pride the first time his son stepped up to the plate in his Little League uniform, or running behind a wobbly little bicycle, or patiently handling the reins of a pony, or…when I imagined him giving that mythical child a gun, I shut my eyes tightly and wished for sleep to wipe away the image.

On the other hand, what if we had a daughter? A dark haired little princess in ruffles and ribbons, gazing up at him in adoration as he told her stories, or stepping out shyly with him at a cotillion, or learning to drive, or watching anxiously as he met her boyfriends and walking the floor waiting for her to return from a date. Perhaps he'd counsel her when she had troubles, or praise her when she did the right thing. I could see his pride as she walked down the aisle in billowing white. I could imagine a tear in his eye as he gave her to another man. In many ways, Javier would be just like my own father. In some ways, he could be better.

"You are smiling, *mi jita*," he mumbled beside me.

I turned to look up at him. "Am I?"

"Is it not so sad anymore?" he asked, his fingers brushing through my hair.

I shook my head. "It was never really sad, Javier."

He drew a deep, labored breath. "I suppose you smile now because we are so close to the border."

"Are we?" I tried to sit up, but he held me still. "How close?"

"I have been giving it some thought. Tomorrow we should be in sight of your rescue. You are nearly home, Dinah."

Home. Where is home, now? It really isn't that big white house with the grape arbor, anymore. Home had become a cave, a jungle path, an open field. Home had become Javier's arms. How could I go back to a place where I no longer belonged? And yet, I have no future here, especially if I am pregnant. I don't really have a right to stay and put that unasked for burden on him. I rested my head against his chest and sighed. Leaving was the saddest thing I could think of.

"Will you think of me?" he asked after a long silence.

I shifted to be closer, listening to the now familiar rhythm of his heartbeat. There was an unvoiced desperation in that question that touched me: the need to be immortal, if only in my dreams. I nearly told him his immortality was already fixed, but I rested my cheek against his and promised, "I think I will always have a little bit of you with me wherever I go, Javier."

Chapter Nine
The Consulate

The next day we got within a mile of the border. We had heard only rumors of the level of involvement by the U.S. government in terms of troops or other aid on the ground, but even from our vantage point we could look south and see battles on the coast, and to the north we could see armed border patrol. Out at sea, large ships with guns waited to be called into action.

Javier hunched on the ground, drawing little maps of the terrain from memory, only to shake his head and scuff away the memory with his foot. "It is worse than I expected," he admitted. "I did not expect the border to be closed yet."

I had found a shady place to sit, and no matter how curious I was, I was too sick and exhausted to move. I lifted a hand to shield my eyes from the afternoon sun. "What do we do?"

"I will think of something," he promised, still dragging his finger through the dirt.

I could see that he was tired, and hot and hungry, and probably still in pain. We had been walking very slowly these last two days, more in consideration for his recent wound than my own condition. I ached for him. It was the first time I had seen him at a loss for a plan, but even so, he still had that fierce determination burning within, that made his features sharp, his brows screwed down into an arrow tip and his mouth an unbreakable line. "Come away from the edge, someone might see you."

I saw his shoulders jerk in a humorless laugh. "And what if they did?" He turned and looked back at me. "It would be better for you, no?"

"To be left up here, alone? No way to get to safety? Is that how little you care?" I suddenly felt irrationally angry and hot tears came quickly.

"No, no, you are right. My duty is to get you to safety." He moved closer to me, and began a new map in the dirt. "If you can come to the edge and see, this white wall that you can see…it seems to be where the U.S. observers are waiting. I have seen many men with binoculars along that wall."

"We're that close?" I pushed myself to my feet, slowly.

"In actual distance, we're very close, but to travel it will take some time. Do you see the American flag? That's where we will go. Do you see the blue and yellow flag next to yours? That is the flag of our country, so our government is already hiding under the American skirts." He sank to the ground in dejection. "Don't go so near the edge. The ground is weak there."

"We could never get through all those soldiers," I said, sinking down beside him.

"The soldiers do not worry me. It is the presence of our government there. I would be arrested and sh-taken prisoner before I could get you safely inside."

I tilted my head toward him. "The government you've fought for would take you prisoner right there, in front of U.S. observers?"

He was quiet for a moment, drawing odd curlicues over the map he had made for me. "At least long enough to get me out of...what do you say..." he tugged at his ear, "that no one can hear?"

"Earshot?"

He nodded and chuckled grimly. "American words sometimes are too accurate."

The meaning of his words struck me hard, and impulsively I threw my arms around him, as if I could pin him to me for all time. "You can't go. I won't let you, Javier."

"It does no for me to go," he agreed, adjusting bedroll into a pillow and easing back. "It still would not mean a safe exit for you. It would only leave you alone up here, or at the mercy of the troops below us." He closed his eyes. "I must think."

I lay down beside him, running my fingers through the many days' growth of blue-black beard. "Isn't there any place we can go, Javier?" I asked wistfully, "just to be together?"

"Do you not want to go home, Dinah?" he asked, his eyes closed, "to your own people, your own bed?"

"You are my people now," I whispered. "I just want to be with you, wherever you are."

He caught my arms and twisted me roughly so that he could glare into my eyes. "Do you not understand? I may not be anywhere tomorrow. Do not give your heart to someone who cannot keep it. I cannot bear to leave you weeping for the rest of your life. Do not do it, Dinah. Do not."

"But, I..."I swallowed back a sob and rushed on with my confession, "I love you, I can't help it. I could never love-"

"Enough." He covered my mouth with his hands. "I am aware of your feelings. I cannot deny my own, no matter how hard I strive to contain them. For that reason, I beg you not to mourn me. Respect my memory, my...feelings for you...respect me enough to keep your feelings private. I do not want your tears as a monument to my life. Promise me that, Dinah. Promise me."

I must have loved him deeply, because he could not have asked a more difficult thing of me and yet, I nodded, brushing away tears and forcing myself to meet his eyes with a calm, if not entirely serene expression. "I promise."

"Thank you." His fingers relaxed around my shoulders, but drew me down against him again. "Now, rest. I must think."

I relaxed against him, actually praying that no idea would come to him, that he would surrender to the hopelessness of his duty and take me to that unknown place where we could live together always.

I woke hours later. It was dark, and cooler than it had been, and I felt stiff, and ill. I sat up and felt around the area where we had been sleeping, and realized I was alone. He had put his jacket over me, and in the pocket I found that little gun he had given me all those weeks ago when he left me in the jungle alone. I want to scream in frustration and despair. Was this his solution – to abandon me in the jungle?

Lying there, staring up at the black sky, I tried to count the stars that winked and blinked above me like something from a Disney film. It all looked beautiful and benign, but it was just as much a fantasy as any story about princesses and happily ever after.

Where had he gone? Was it the hopelessness I had prayed for him to see that drove him away? Was he frightened by something? Had he simply tired of his responsibility? I didn't believe any of those ideas. Javier had thought the situation through and now he was acting on those thoughts. But what had he decided to do?

Sleep was impossible, so I remained still, frightened by every sound that the hostile world around me made; every crack, swish or snap could be a deadly animal or a poisonous viper or a vicious solder. I stayed so still that my muscles ached and seized so that I couldn't move at all. My life was, at that moment, a hundred times worse than my worst nightmare.

My father had always taught me that when I was frightened I should think of a happy thought, a wonderful memory. I had so many to choose from; there was the day when Javier and I had found that hidden grove of flowers and mossy grass and we were both so overwhelmed by the beauty and peacefulness of the place that we forgot to be on guard. We made love, and talked – not just whispered, but talked in full voice about secret hurts and dreams and then succumbing to passion again. There day we found the abandoned wildcat cubs and despite his dire warnings, my attempts to play with them drew Javier into the game, until we heard gunfire nearby and had to scramble for a hiding place. There was the last day at our honeymoon retreat and the tenderness with which he made love to me, the fierceness with which he schooled me in passion.

There was, too, the knowledge that, although he would never confess it outright, Javier loved me and, best of all, that I would have his child.

What kind of life could we give a child if we chose to run and hide? Not a very good one. He'd never know the stability of a home; he'd never have a puppy, a swing, a bicycle, a room full of toys or a Christmas tree. He'd never go to school, and have lifelong friends. But, if I left Javier, he'd never have a father. He'd never know his father was a man of strength and dignity, a moral man in the midst of an immoral conflict.

Suddenly there was a rustle nearby, breaking my thoughts in little pieces of fear. Trying to be invisible in the darkness, I inched my hand into the pocket where he had hidden the gun. The movement was definitely caused by a man, even the largest jungle animal had a much lighter step. But, who? Was it Javier, returning to me from wherever he had gone? Was it a deserter from the front about to discover me? Should I shoot? Could I? Eyes fixed on the darkness, I waited until the movement closer to me. I didn't scream, though I wanted to, but I eased the gun from the pocket and aimed it.

The figure moved into the clearing just a foot or two from me, hunched over and cautious. The moon seemed unwilling to reveal his face, but I knew that silhouette, those broad shoulders and slim hips. I knew every detail because I had slept beside that figure every night for weeks. "Javier?"

A small beam of light flicked on and flashed in my direction. "Dinah, *soy yo*,"

I sighed and lowered the gun. "I was so scared," I admitted.

He knelt beside me. "I did not think you would wake or would have told you I was leaving and called out to you when I returned." He eased the gun out my clenched fingers. "I am very grateful you were brave enough to call out to me before shooting. I think if I had taken one more step you would have dealt me the same fate as my attacker." He patted his side.

I sat up and reached for him. "Where were you? Where did you go?"

He pulled me into an embrace and stroked my hair. "I have made arrangements."

"Arrangements?" No, not now. One more day, please? Just one more day. "How?"

"I have made contact with the government officials across the border. They will-"

"Oh, Javier, no!"

He put a silencing finger on my lips. "Not directly, *querida*. I sent a..." he frowned, as he always did when looking for an English word, "an emissary. The government will be informed that I am holding a hostage and that I want to exchange that hostage for my safe passage to Nicaragua. I have given them your name and made certain that your parents will be notified. When all is agreed and in place we will get a message. "

"I don't like this," I said, shaking my head. "What if this emissary betrays you?"

He smiled, but it was a cold smile. "He will not."

"How can you be sure? Everyone's allegiances seem to change every day here."

"He is my brother," Javier answered tersely. "He once had a farm near here, and he continues to live nearby in the hope of the land being returned to him. And yet, blood is still more binding that politics."

"Oh." I settled down against him. I didn't realize he had a brother – at least not a living one. There was so much about him I did not know and there was no time left to learn. "What will happen in Nicaragua?"

He shrugged against me. "Nothing. I will not go to Nicaragua. I made no arrangements for my safe arrival."

"Clever," I said doubtfully.

"Not so clever, *mi jita*, or I would have found a way to keep you with me always."

"I could keep you with me," I suggested. "You could return with me to the U.S."

He silenced me this time with his lips. "No more talk, *mi esposa*, we have too little moonlight left."

Manuel Contreras came in the late of evening of the next day. All day Javier had been on edge, pacing, crouching to look down at the border below. It was strangely quiet below us, not a single sound of battle could be heard; it felt as if there was something in the air, some anticipation, as if the world was holding its collective breath. I could not get near enough to Javier to soothe either of us. At dawn, he told me that we could no longer be man and wife. He had removed himself from me, his eyes never strayed to me, his voice crisp and commanding when he spoke at all.

When Manuel arrived, a small, less handsome version of Javier, Javier pulled out his gun and kept it leveled at him throughout the conversation of rapid fire Spanish. Even though I couldn't understand any of the exchange, I understood why Javier felt the need to be armed. Manuel did not wear even the tattered remnants of a uniform; he wore baggy, dirty pants, a nondescript green blouse and the leather huaraches that peasants wore. Manuel Contreras was a rebel, or a rebel sympathizer. How galling it must have been for Javier to seek his help to get me to safety.

He turned to me at last, his eyes falling over me, warmly, for only a moment before he gestured sharply for me to stand. I obeyed, moving toward the two men, uncertainly. He made a twisting motion with his hand, bidding me to turn around, slowly, as if to assure Manuel that I was unharmed. I did so, feeling Manuel's eyes on me with the same look I had seen so often when we were in camp.

Javier spoke again to Manuel, hissing his words through clenched teeth. Manuel answered leeringly, causing Javier's fingers to tighten on the gun in his hand. Instead of firing, Javier jerked the gun in the direction Manuel had come and, with a grunt, the brother left.

I remained where I was, watching Javier from the corner of my eye. He just stood there, staring after Manuel, his fingers clenched around the grip of the gun. Finally, he turned. "Tomorrow," he said, tersely.

I swallowed and nodded. I wanted to argue, I ached to argue, but I knew the tremendous sacrifice he had made for me. "Tomorrow," I repeated.

Javier looked to the ground. "The Peace Corps notified your father after the insurrection. He has been waiting in *Cuidad de Mexico* for some word from you. Manuel will get word back to the Embassy to let him know that you are alive and unharmed."

"Oh, thank God." I was ashamed that I had not even thought of my parents' anguish in weeks.

He stiffened and raised his eyes to mine. "I am sorry that he has suffered all this time not knowing if you had lived or died." He returned to his post at the edge of the cliff, his back to me.

"I'm sorry, too," I confessed, "but I'm not sorry that I met you."

He turned slightly and saw that same anguish in his eyes. "Do not do this to me, *querida*," he implored. After a moment, he added, "Get some sleep. Tomorrow will be a hard day for everyone.""

I tried to sleep, but rest evaded me. I understood Javier's restlessness as he paced the ground nearby, unable to come near me and sleep. It was as if he was already dead.

I spent that night reliving every moment with him, even those terrible first days when my fate was so uncertain, when I stood up to him for a freedom he had tried to strip from me, for a pride he was trying to crush.

I would always remember his haughty arrogance, his evil intentions, his impatient demands, and then I would temper those memories with his humble surrender the night he gave me a battered green cap, his name and, I believe, his love.

I would always remember his gentleness, his understanding, his protective nature. I would remember his pride and the respect that he commanded from his men, the authority with which he moved. I would always remember his sometimes seemingly heartless wisdom, and I would remember his compassion. This was the legacy he would give to his child – a child he would never know.

I sat up in the darkness, my hand over my abdomen. I couldn't take that child away without his knowledge. I had to tell him.

I searched for him. He stood near the ledge looking down at the field we would cross to get to the border. That ledge would slice us apart ad swallow us up into two different worlds. "Javier?"

He didn't turn around. "Go to sleep, Dinah," he murmured.

"But, Javier, I-"

He turned toward the horizon, hands clasped behind his back. With the faint light of the moon, I could see him in profile. His expression was like stone. "It will be dawn soon. There is a long day ahead. You need your rest."

I stared at him, willing him to turn around, to show me one ounce of feeling. He did not move. "But, Javier, there is something I must tell you."

"I will not listen to you, Dinah," he said savagely. "*Por Dios*, be merciful."

"But, Javier."

"*¡Cállate!*" he thundered and the command echoed out over the battlefield and back, hollow, angry, hurt.

I swallowed back any further protest, and turned away from him, as tears burned my eyes

"Dinah."

I turned, blindly. It was barely dawn, and I hadn't slept at all. My eyes were swollen and burning and my stomach rolled dangerously.

"It is time." His voice was taut and withdrawn.

I nodded and moved, reluctantly. My back and legs ached, my heart was heavy. I hated the way I felt, knowing this is the way he would remember me: dirty, uncombed and sick. I staggered to my feet. "I'm ready."

"I brought you water," he said, abruptly. "I do not want the Americans to think that you suffered unduly." He indicated a pan of water resting on a rock. Beside it were the remnants of that precious bar of Ivory soap.

I wanted to fly into his arms and smother him with my gratitude. Instead, I nodded my thanks and knelt before my makeshift bath.

With Javier standing guard, his back to me, I stripped off my shirt and scrubbed every inch I could reach. When I reached for my shirt, I found it wasn't there.

"No, Dinah, take this." He had turned around, holding out a white cotton undershirt. His eyes went over me as he held it out, and then he looked away.

I was hurt enough by his refusal to look at me that I didn't wonder where he had managed to find a clean shirt after so many weeks away from such luxuries as baths and laundry. As I tried to arrange the shirt in such a way that it didn't hang on me like a parachute, I realized that my body had probably changed quite a lot since our first encounter. My arms and legs were thin, my collar bone stuck out, my knuckles were swollen, making my hands look deformed. There were places which were rounder than before, but he didn't seem to notice them. "All right, I'm dressed."

He turned, and his eyes dropped down over me and I know he saw everything from haggard expression to tear filled eyes. He nodded and bent to collect the green cap. "Do not forget this, Dinah," he said. With fingers so skilled one would think it was a practiced gesture, he lifted my hair from my neck and coiled it on top of my head before placing the cap on top and tugging it into place.

"But, I'm leaving," I protested, reaching to remove the hat. "This is yours."

He stopped my hand. "I gave it to you, Dinah. It would be meaningless to have it now." He jerked a thumb in the direction of the ledge. "Go and keep watch while I break the camp."

I sat on the tree stump which had served as my chair for three days, watching him carefully sort through the items strewn about as he prepared my bag with what was left of my belongings. His fingers brushed over the small, silver framed photograph. The look he gave the picture was one of such longing that I stood, impulsively, taking the frame and slipping the picture out of it. I tucked into the pocket of his shirt. "To remember me?" I asked, wistfully.

He nodded and returned to his task.

I returned to the tree stump and looked into the valley.

"I wish I had something to give you to remember me, and our time together, Dinah," he said, after a few moments.

"Oh, Javier," I said on a long and painful sigh, "if you only knew."

Javier returned to his work with a dogged determination, his mouth screwed up into a frown. Suddenly, his hands still, but he did not look up. "When my brother returns, you must remember your place; you must act as my prisoner. There can be no parting for us. You will..." his hand flicked toward the direction Manuel had come the night before, "go." He lifted his head and sought my eyes at last. "Do you understand?"

I nodded, but I did not understand.

He saw the bewilderment in my eyes and he shifted his weight, my bag still in his hands. "If anyone suspects that you are anything but a prisoner of war being...being..." he scowled in frustration, "repatriated, your life would be nothing." He made a slicing gesture with one hand. "It would be made to be an accident, of course, but they would take your life to punish me. Remember as you cross that valley, Dinah, that you are going through a battlefield, walking with a thousand guns pointed at you and no one to shield you. Do nothing to endanger yourself."

Now I understood.

When Manuel returned, he came with two other men. They all greeted Javier with contempt, one of them drawing a long, deadly looking blade from his waistband.

Javier responded to the threat by jerking me up from the tree stump and pressing his gun against my temple. The fear I displayed wasn't feigned. I didn't want to go. I was terrified of leaving him; leaving him to his fate, and going toward my own. But, I could see in their eyes that they were afraid to lose the bounty they would receive for getting me safely across the border. Manuel muttered something to the man with the knife and the weapon was thrust back into his belt.

There was another exchange of that rapid fire Spanish that was beyond my skills, and Manuel pointed toward the trail, barely discerned in the early morning light, which worked down the side of the mountain and across the valley. Javier, with his arm still tight around my waist and arm, leaned forward to consider the path before he nodded his approval.

Manuel and his companions stood back and allowed Javier to direct me toward the ledge.

I hesitated, looking down the steep descent. I would surely stumble at least once during that walk, and that would leave Javier vulnerable to the men behind him. Javier pushed at me, impatiently. "Move," he hissed.

I began to cry. It wasn't entirely for show, but it was earnest enough to be effective. "Make them go first," I wept, hoping that their English was not good enough to understand through a woman's weeping.

Javier stepped back from the ledge, pulling me back as well. He barked a command that was discussed and debated. When it looked as if they would not comply, he calmly raised the barrel of the gun to my head once again. I could hear the horrible metallic ping of a bullet falling under the firing pin. Javier's hand didn't even tremble.

I started crying even louder.

Our three companions exchanged more words and then shuffled past us, their eyes fixed on Javier's hand until the uneven path forced them to look down. Javier waited until they were too far down to turn around and charge us, and then squeezed my arm as he lowered his gun.

He spoke soft encouragement as he directed me toward the valley, but I wasn't listening. All that mattered to me was that those three men were ahead of us, and that would give Javier a few precious moments to disappear while all eyes were on me.

It took a long time to get down that rocky path. The sun was high above us when we reached the valley floor. I could not see any soldiers, but I had no doubt they were there. Suddenly, Manuel stopped in front of us and drew his own gun. I would have screamed if Javier had not covered my mouth with his hand. He raised his gun, too, and this time I could see the tiniest tremor in his hand as he once again pressed it against my temple.

Manuel fired into the air. There was a blinding red flare and I watched its path in horror and fascination. The shooting stopped.

The abrupt silence was eerie. There was death in the air. I could smell it. It was thick and rancid. I could almost hear the last gasps of life just a few yards away from us. I shuddered against Javier.

Ahead of us on that path crudely cleared of vegetation by machete, a Jeep rolled into view and stopped. I had seen the battle lines as we had come down the mountain, I had seen the building, like a tall, white enrobed nun just beyond. It was the US Embassy in Guatemala and, if Javier's brother was telling the truth, my father was waiting for me, there.

I should have longed to break free and run to him, to my Daddy who could make everything right, who could return me to the life I'd known only a few months ago, but in reality, I wanted to remain in the embrace of the man who had given me his name, his life, his child. "Javier, I'm pregnant," I tried to tell him but my words came out a strangled sob.

Javier's grip slackened as Manuel and the others moved toward the Jeep. His gun no longer touched me. Finally, it was only one hand rested on my shoulder as if he meant to steady me. I turned to look at him, to repeat my confession, to make sure he knew he had left a greater impression on the future than he could have ever hoped, but he jerked me forward roughly. "Do not look at me, Dinah," he insisted. "I cannot bear to say goodbye to you."

"Then don't," I answered. It seemed so simple to me. Come with me, be safe, be an American with me.

"Dinah," he implored.

I couldn't bear to hear the break in his voice so I nodded and said nothing else while we waited there, at the edge of death.

He must have seen some signal that I could not perceive for, finally, his hand slipped away from me and he stepped back. "Go, Dinah," he said, harshly. "Go and do not look back, no matter what you hear."

I swallowed hard, steeling myself not to turn back into his arms. My feet felt like lead. "I can't," I whispered.

"Go," he commanded, "and go bravely. Let me remember you as worthy of my name."

I lifted my head, faced the path ahead, took a deep breath and began to walk. He had always said he admired my strength of spirit, my bravery. I wanted him to be proud of me now. This was the hardest, most frightening thing I had ever done. Impulsively, I paused long enough to look up into the dusty, yellow sky. Oh, God, let him be proud of me for a long, long time.

As I passed the Jeep, I faltered. There the path had widened, a road cut by bullets. I knew there were snipers in the tall grass on both sides. I could see the dead and dying dragged to the sides of the road, I could see that I would walk over the pools of blood where they had fallen. I could never have imagined a nightmare like this. I wanted to turn around and run back to Javier, but I knew he was already gone. "Via con Dios," I murmured, and began to walk again, slowly at first, and then a little faster. I imagined that my father was among those waiting at the end of the road. As I began to distinguish features of the stern looking men in the row of Jeeps at the other end of the road, the

Jeeps with familiar flags fluttering in the deathless air, I began to run. I felt Javier's cap fly off and my hair spill down wildly over my shoulders. I didn't stop to pick it up, but my heart was left back there in the trampled grass and I mourned the loss of both.

I'm not exactly certain where I crossed the border, but fifty feet from the row of Jeeps I could see him, despite the fact that my eyes were so filled with tears I could hardly make my way. My father stood up and, restrained from climbing out of the Jeep by one of the soldiers with him, held out his arms to me.

Suddenly, I was surrounded by men in khaki and hustled toward the row of Jeeps, as other soldiers trained their rifles on the battlefield behind me. The Jeep onto which I was lifted was already backing up, ready to withdraw into the safety of the Embassy. I struggled to sit up and scanned the scene, looking for some sign of Javier, even if it was an indication that he had been captured...or killed.

As the gates clanged shut, Daddy scrambled out of his Jeep and rushed to me, gathering me against his chest too tightly, stroking my hair, sobbing against my cheek. "Oh, baby, we didn't think we would ever see you again. Dinah, Dinah, baby, we've been so scared."

I clung to him, in desperation and grief, wanting him to erase this memory, this pain, but this was one pain he couldn't kiss and make better. This was one nightmare he couldn't ever take away. He could never take away the horror of death and hatred and revenge. He couldn't make me stop reliving scene after scene of incredible brutality.

There was no my gentle and genteel father could understand that Javier had a man shot before my eyes because he dared put his hands on a woman Javier desired.

There was no way my father, born to privilege and ease, could understand the hopelessness I had known when I returned to that filthy hovel and found that poor baby gone and his mother going.

There was no way my father, who believed in peace and good will between all men, could comprehend my blinding need for survival that enabled me to pull the trigger of a gun and kill a man who threatened Javier's life and would, ultimately, threatened mine.

There was nothing my daddy could do, nothing he could say and nothing he could buy to replace the loss of innocence I had experienced. As I rested in the comfort of his embrace, within the stone walls of the Embassy, I felt I had lost everything.

I had lost enough, I suppose. When I stepped off that train only a few months ago, I struggled with three suitcases, a bag full of medical books, a heart full of hope and a head full of idealism. As I stumbled out of the Jeep in the Embassy courtyard, I had a small, Spanish language Bible and the empty picture frame. But, it wasn't the possessions I mourned. It wasn't even the loss of my hope, my idealism, or my faith in mankind. I had lost even more than that.

Just this morning I had lost my husband, my lover, the father of my child. I'd lost my sense of individuality. I would never be my own person again. I would always be a part of this jungle, this dirty, dusty, stinking, sweltering, cheating place I had learned to see as Paradise.

There was a pop of gunfire somewhere beyond the gates and people around me scrambled for defensive positions. Daddy tried to pull me toward a door in the wall behind us, but I had turned back, in horror. In those months I had learned to gauge the distance of gunfire and that was a long way off…on the other side of the border. I could feel the bullet pierce me as if I had been standing there beside him. How could I have imagined, or even dared dream that Javier would be so overwhelmed by his love for me that he would rush headlong into the gun sights of a thousand men who had sworn to see him dead? Yet, as I raced toward the door my father was beckoning me to, I was still listening for the sound of his boots behind me.

There was no answering fire. There was silence, as if the battle awaited some signal from this side of the border to resume. I paused at the door and looked down through the gates to the path I had just crossed, where the dust of my footsteps still swirled in the air. What were they waiting for? Were they planning to drag his body to the gates, a trophy for the old government to admire? Would I be exposed to that? I shut my eyes and tried to turn away, but I couldn't. I would have to know, I would have to see him.

Daddy wrapped his arm around my shoulder, and squeezed. "I can't believe you're safe," he said, breathlessly. "You're okay."

When I opened my eyes, I was surrounded by people: soldiers in khaki, men in suits, men in the pompous uniforms of the former government, and

Guatemalan officials. They were pressing in on me, trying to capture my attention, demanding a piece of me. I looked at them all helplessly from the haven of my father's arms. Time seemed to be suspended; although I could see mouths moving and hands gesturing, no comprehendible sound reached me. It was as if I no longer understood English.

"*Senorita* McKee! *Senorita* McKee! You are unharmed?"

"Believe me, this *Capitan* Contreras will pay for this outrage!"

"Miss McKee, do you need medical attention?"

"Miss McKee, do you know where the rest of his regiment is camped?"

"*Senorita*, come this way. We have a bed for you."

What I could hear, and understand, was the rattling of machine guns as the conflict resumed, out there.

Chapter Ten
The Conclusion

There were a million questions thrown at me in the next few days. I answered them all with the patient litany, "I 'm fine, I'm really fine. I do not know where they are, I don't know where he went. I don't know their plans."

I stayed three days at the Embassy, during which time the sound of battle faded into the distance. I was given a cursory examination by a doctor there, and fortunately for me, he only wanted to report good news to his superiors so he reported that I was in remarkably good condition considering my recent captivity, and never even guessed at the secrets I kept.

We spent another three days in Mexico City, with more official hovering, more insistent questions, and my first encounter with global media. Newspapers were filled with details of the conflict, and the United States' recent involvement. Reporters gathered around the hotel, hoping to get some kind of statement from me. I met with some members of Military Intelligence who didn't believe me when I said I knew nothing about Javier's plans. They became so insistent that Daddy threatened to get an attorney.

I was exhausted. I couldn't eat. I couldn't go outside my hotel room without an escort. I couldn't sleep for fear of nightmares and I couldn't go home until the assorted government agencies 'cleared' me. Oh, I pretended to be fine. I smiled, and made a great show of enjoying the food sent to my room every day. I even pretended to sleep every night, knowing that Daddy was coming into my room to sit by my bed, the way he used to do when I was frightened by a storm. I could never lower my guard, or let my smile slip. I felt as if I was going to shatter.

A week after Javier had pushed me out into that pathway between two warring states, I was allowed to go home. We flew home in a nearly empty First Class section. I sat next to the window and watched the mountains south of Mexico City disappear into clouds.

Beside me, Daddy shifted and sighed. I knew that he had questions, but I didn't give him an opening. I continued to stare out the window. I knew that I wasn't behaving like a woman overjoyed by her rescue, grateful to go home. I knew it bewildered and hurt him, but I didn't have it in me to reassure him.

We were crossing over the Gulf before he sighed again, loudly, and twisted toward me. "Your mother will be so relieved to see you, "he said, tentatively. "It was very hard on her, your decision."

"Mmm," I mumbled.

"And this experience," he hesitated, "it is going to be very painful for her to see that..."

I turned slightly, not meeting his eyes, but granting permission for him to continue."

He sighed again. "I haven't wanted to press you, but I can see that something happened, that something terrible happened, something that you can't talk about-"

"No, I cannot," I answered sharply. "So please, stop."

I heard him suck in breath in surprise. "Baby," he said, after a moment. "Can't you tell me what happened? You know nothing can change how I feel – how we feel about you."

"Daddy," I tried to soften my tone to match his, "I just can't. Not now. Not yet."

I felt him turn in his seat and I knew I had hurt him, but telling him what was on my mind would hurt him more.

A stewardess brought a cart to our row, but I had returned to my view of the clouds and water beneath us. I was surprised, therefore, when my father set a small glass in front of me. "Brandy," he said with no further explanation.

I stared at the glass as if it were Holy water.

He sipped from his own glass. "Yes, your mother is thrilled beyond words that you're finally coming home."

Finally? "I wasn't gone that long," I said, petulantly.

"To us, it seemed like forever." He sipped again. "When we heard about the revolution, naturally we made inquiries through the Peace Corps and then US Embassy. We were told, both times, that the Corps had been removed from the country. We expected you home in a matter of days, then." He paused, leaving room for me to fill in the blanks.

"Yes." I ran a fingertip around the edge of the plastic glass. "We were told to evacuate." I shrugged. "Actually, the militia was throwing us out."

Daddy seemed encouraged by my response. "When I heard that, I flew down to Mexico City. That's where we were told to expect you. A special plane, they said..." there was an uncharacteristic quiver to his voice. "They said that there was no other plane, and no other survivors."

My heart wrenched. I had been so selfish! In my grief, I never even considered what they had gone through. "I missed the train," I explained quickly. "There was a heavily pregnant woman." I faltered and quickly gulped from the glass in front of me. He didn't need to know all the circumstances.

"And?" he prompted.

I kept my eyes on the glass in my fingers. The brandy rippled as my fingers trembled. "The village was overrun – by rebels, by militia, I don't know. I just had to get out."

He did not say anything, but he practically vibrated with unasked questions. When I did not amplify my explanation, he said, "When so much time went by, people began to suggest that I go home, that we give up hope. The Peace Corps and Governor McKeithen both offered to arrange memorial services."

I wondered if anyone would perform a memorial service for Javier.

"Your mother refused to give up. She said a mother would know if her child were dead and she didn't know that. So I kept flying back to Mexico City, knocking on doors, making phone calls, being a general nuisance. The Ambassador there began a push to recover-" he stopped and emptied his glass. "When I got the call to come down to the Embassy in Guatemala, they wouldn't tell me why. I fully expected to be told..."

"That they had found my body?" I looked up, focusing on his words again. "No, Daddy, I'm not shocked. I'm not even surprised. Sometimes it seems more shocking that I'm still alive."

"Why would you say that, Dinah?" He reached for my hand and squeezed it. "How did you survive?

He was asking more questions than I wanted to answer. There were answers I had not revealed, even during the debriefing with both members of both governments. I pushed my glass away. I would never drink brandy again. "People helped me. The militia was afraid of repercussions from the American government if something happened to me. There was a Captain...Contreras." I was proud that my voice didn't break as I said his name. "He made it his duty to get me to the border alive."

Daddy nodded. "It was evident that a lot of different parties were involved in the effort. There were a lot of preparations. I didn't know until just before it took place that you were actually crossing between two armies. I thought I was going to die of fear-"

"Daddy," I put a hand on his, "I'm a little tired. Wake me when we get to New Orleans." I leaned back and shut my eyes.

When I awoke, we were on the tarmac of New Orleans International, and there were people with balloons and signs bearing my name gathered below the plane. "What's all this?" I asked my father.

"A heroine's welcome," he answered with a smile.

"I'm not a heroine, nothing like it!" I protested, but Daddy just kept smiling.

There was a phalanx of news reporters, with microphones waving and flashbulbs popping, crowded around the arrival gate. I must have flinched once too often because my gentle father got angry and called them all ghouls, ushering me away under the cover of his jacket. Questions and cameras followed us all the way to the taxi stand and I felt I could still hear them even as we pulled away from the curb.

We rode in silence for a long time, but as we passed out of Jefferson Parish, I turned to my father impulsively. "Did you trim the arbor this year?"

If my question surprised him, he hid it well. "I had to. We had a bumper crop of grapes."

"And did Mom make jelly?"

Daddy smiled. "Jars and jars."

I settled back against the seat. "I missed Mom's jelly so much. Sometimes I think that's the only thing that got me through."

I could hear my parents talking about me, as I sat near the door of my bedroom that night. For some reason I couldn't rest in my soft bed, so I sat on the floor, with my door open an inch or two, just to see the lights flickering on the familiar white columns that rose up from the foyer, and to hear the reassuring sound of my parents' voices just across the landing.

"She looks terrible," my mother said. Her voice didn't wobble, but then, Mom has been always pragmatic. "She's so thin, she looks so frail."

"Well, she's been through quite an ordeal," Daddy answered.

"I never thought my daughter would have an ordeal," Mom responded, grimly. "But, it's more than that. She tries to be bright and positive and untouched, but she's hiding something terrible from us."

"We don't know that," Daddy protested.

"No, we do. I do. A mother knows."

"Let's give her some time…a few days to feel at home again."

They were quiet for a time, and I strained to hear their words. At last Mom spoke again. "David, have you considered that she might have been tortured, perhaps…" I could hear her struggle to say the word none of us wanted her to say, "raped?"

"The doctors didn't mention it, and she hasn't said anything," Daddy insisted. "I thought that was a good sign."

"She might be trying to protect us," Mom said, gently, as if trying to protect my father. "Or maybe it all seems like a terrible dream and she expects to wake up and find everything is back to normal. But, I know my daughter, and I know she's been wounded, terribly wounded, and sooner or later, she is going to tell us what happened. We need to be prepared not to react and make her feel worse."

That was so typical of my mother, and why I loved her so much.

As much as I loved my parents I couldn't tolerate being imprisoned by the walls my home. Though my mother kept urging me to stay in my bed and rest, I had to be up and on the move. I wandered my neighborhood, expecting it to have undergone monumental changes in my absence, but while the place did seem different, it was me who had changed. I went to the local shopping center, and ran through the park where I had played as a child, reliving memories. None of the places I went, none of the memories I conjured could paint over the images that had been etched in my thoughts.

When that failed, I did retreat to my bed, in my darkened room, declining invitations to visit friends or come downstairs to eat with my parents. With the lights off in my bedroom, I hoped I could shut off all the longing and fear that I had brought home with me. That failed, as well. Finally, I couldn't put it off any longer and went downstairs to find my parents.

They were in the family room, by the fire, whispering worriedly over their coffee. They both looked up, almost guiltily, when I pushed the doors aside and stood in front of them. "Mom, Daddy, I have to tell you something."

Mom rose halfway from her chair, as if fighting her urge to come to me. Daddy folded his newspaper and put his coffee cup down with deliberation. "Yes, Dinah?"

I took a deep breath. Javier wanted me to be brave. It made him proud. I wondered, briefly, if he would be proud of me now for what I was about to do. I didn't want to wonder if he was even capable of being proud anymore. I had watched the news, and there were reports of heavy casualties on both sides, but no word of his fate. Of course he was dead, I would be a fool to hope otherwise, but he would never be gone. I would always have him, carried under my heart.

Yet, as I opened my mouth to reveal my secret to my parents, my strength failed me. All I could do was stumble and stammer as my eyes went around the familiar room. It should have been my haven, the safest place in the world, with the two people who loved me above all else, but that love and safety were no match to the truth I was about to tell.

Mom stood at last and held out her hand. "Come sit down, Dinah. Would you like some coffee?"

I couldn't get closer to them, not until they knew what had happened, and I knew how they would react. They would be angry, of course. It was their duty to be angry about anything that happened to me. Would they also be angry that I accepted what happened and that I wanted it to go on and on? How could I explain it? How could I make them understand? There was no delicate way to phrase the unavoidable facts. "Mom, Daddy, I'm pregnant."

I sat up in my bed, watching the tiny arms and legs wave and kick from within the wicker bassinet, while Mom fussed with a bottle. "You're just like your father," I whispered. "He was demanding and impatient, too."

Mom turned toward me, a towel at her wrist to wipe away formula. "Did you say something, dear?" To the casual observer, her expression and tone of voice would never betray the strain between us now.

"No, I was talking to Jay." I knew it was hard on Mom and Daddy to deal with all of this. An unwed mother was shocking enough, but when I refused to give any details about the father, and they could only presume to understand the background, it was beyond even their broadminded compassion to be happy that I had chosen to keep the child. I reached into the bassinet and stroked his little fingers. "He seems to like hearing my voice."

Mom brought the bottle to me and I tried to school the disappointment from my face. The doctor had said that my state of malnutrition early in the pregnancy had rendered me unable to nurse Jay. I struggled into a sitting position and Mom lifted Jay into my arms. "Dinah," she began, hesitantly, but changed her mind and handed me the little blue towel, as well.

"Mom, I know that look, and I know what you're going to say," I said, urging the nipple toward that little bow shaped pout. "I haven't changed my mind. I'm not going to change my mind, so please, don't try."

"But, Dinah," she protested, even though her expression was both angry and ashamed.

I took a sharp, deep breath so Jay wouldn't feel my body go rigid in irritation. "I will not give him up. Can't you see?" I looked down into Jay's little face, as he worked at the nipple, fiercely. His skin was so dark next to mine. "I went down there to do some good – just as I was raised to do. I went down there to save lives. That's why I became a nurse. If this is the only good I can do, then it is what I do. Jay is my son, he is your grandson, and that is the end of the discussion."

Mom turned away. It took me a moment to realize that I had moved her to tears. I began to word an apology that wouldn't weaken my earlier statement, but she turned back to me, her face red, her eyes wet with tears. "But to bear the child of some filthy, heathen rebel," she burst out in protest, "to have to live with the memory of all those months as a captive in the jungle." A violent shudder ripped through her. "Beaten and r-raped and abused." She sank to the edge of the bed, sobbing.

As much as I wanted to keep my heartache to myself, seeing my mother suffer from such notions forced me to cast off my silences. "Mother, whoever said I was beaten and raped and abused?"

She gaped at me and, after a moment, gestured faintly toward Jay.

I sighed. "Mom, would it comfort you at all to know that Jay's father saved my lie? That he was a God fearing Catholic, and he wasn't filthy by any definition of the word?" Would it comfort you to know his most prized possession may well have been a bar of Ivory soap? My heart swelled a little at that little memory.

"Then...you know who the father was?"

"Mom." I hated surrendering my secret, but I hated making my mother cry even more. "I was married to Jay's father. Yes, married, in front of a priest. It was in a tent in the middle of the jungle, but it was official. There was a witness. There were vows. And...and I loved him. He loved me, I think, in his own way."

Mom looked at me, blinking slowly, absorbing my confession. "My God," she whispered hoarsely. She looked at Jay and then swallowed hard. "My God," she repeated. She seemed to see me in a different way, suddenly. "No wonder you didn't want to talk about it. I knew you were in pain, but I never thought… where is he?"

I struggled not to let my voice break. "He's probably dead. He traded his life and freedom to get me to the Embassy." I shifted Jay in my arms. I wanted to cry, but I'd promised Javier that I would never mourn him publicly and I was going to keep that promise.

"Then he doesn't know…" she stopped. "He doesn't know you made it home safely?"

I knew she was really asking if he knew about Jay. I smiled. "I think he knows, somehow."

"He should be very proud of his beautiful son."

"Mom, you surprise me. A moment ago you were angrily opposed to him – even more so than Daddy."

Mom smiled in contrition. "No mother likes to see her child suffer," she said, standing to come nearer. "You'll understand someday." She patted my shoulder. "All I saw was suffering, and of course I opposed that. When all I had was the belief that his father was some nameless animal who attacked my daughter in the jungles of a war-torn country how could I have anything but opposition? I knew the minute you laid eyes on that child, you would be looking that animal in the face again." She reached for the baby, tenderly, and bounced him gently in her arms. It was the first time she had held Jay and tears of relief replaced my grief, and spilled down my face, unchecked. It was a sight I'd never thought I'd see.

"That's why I agreed to a home birth," she continued, making faces at the baby. "I was afraid, during labor, you...you would..."

"Let it all out?" I filled in.

"I did expect some kind of breakdown," she admitted. "I didn't want that to happen in some cold, sterile institution. When I heard the baby cry and the midwife came out to tell us it was a boy, I ran in here expecting you to be hysterical, but you were joyful, thankful, relieved...happy. I didn't understand that you felt exactly the way I did when you were born. If I had I would have been more supportive of you throughout the pregnancy."

"It's not your fault. I just wasn't ready to tell anyone."

"A mother should know." She patted my cheek. "It's finally cooling off. Why don't you take the baby down to the garden for a while? It will be good for both of you. You've been cooped up in this room for far too long."

"In a little while, Mom, I promise."

It took me a few days to force myself out of my safe little cocoon. I didn't want to meet with neighbors, or risk any more reporters, especially with Jay in my arms, but Mom argued that I'd been home long enough I was no longer the nine day wonder of the parish. The arbor was heavy with purple fruit, and the last of the summer flowers filled the garden with all the promises I had made to herself during the early days with Javier.

Mom brought me a glass of iced and a shawl – only a mother would do that. "Daddy's late harvesting the grapes," I observed, sitting forward so she could drape the crocheted wrap across my shoulders. "We're not going to have any jelly this year, if he doesn't hurry. Where is he, anyway? I don't think I've seen him in days."

My mom looked toward the house. "I don't know...he's been working on some project for a few days. Everything is hush-hush, I guess. Every time I go near the study I can hear him on the telephone, and when I go in, he stops talking." She shrugged. "If I didn't know him so well, I'd think he was seeing another woman."

"Not Daddy!" I laughed.

"No, not Daddy," she agreed, and leaned over to kiss my cheek. "Don't stay out too long. I know, I know, I'm the one who has been pushing you to go out, but I know your tendency to overdo."

"We won't," I promised and settled back in the chaise, thumbing through a magazine with disinterest. I didn't know what was wrong with me. This was my home, my heart realized. I was safe, I was with people who loved and cared for me. I was in my grape arbor, with the family cat curled up at the foot of the lounge. Yet, I felt restless, useless, unfinished. My son deserved more. I needed to go back to work. Obviously, the Peace Corps wouldn't be possible, not with a baby in tow, but some organization must need a good nurse with field experience.

I put the magazine down and closed my eyes, listening to the electric buzz of humming birds, and the faint sounds of children and traffic at the end of the avenue. When I heard the front door bell echo through the kitchen window, I picked up the magazine and began to turn pages again, wrinkling my nose at poufy hairstyles coming into fashion.

The kitchen door opened, and I glanced up and turned a page. Then I looked up again, in disbelief. I looked at the commercial for mascara in front of me, something real and tangible and possible, and then up at the doorway, my mouth going dry, realizing that I was hallucinating. Heart in my throat, I sat up, trying to speak. I could see Mom peering out the kitchen window.

He looked tired, he looked thin, and he looked out of place in clean, pressed blue jeans and a striped polo shirt, but his limbs appeared to be intact and there were no visible scars or injuries. And he was alive! "Javier," I croaked, at last, searching blindly for a place to put the magazine down, and finally let it go, and it fell to the ground. "You said you wouldn't come. You said..." my voice failed me and I struggled to find it again. "You said that the war came first."

For the first time, the arrogance in his expression gave way to uncertainty. He hovered in the doorway, as if unsure of his welcome. "Dinah," he said roughly, "the war is over." He sent his eyes around the patio the way he used to scan the fields for snipers.

"I'm so relieved for you." I dropped the shawl and rose with an embarrassing lack of grace. I wanted to rush into his arms, but the way he stood, so rigid, so withdrawn, I didn't feel welcome. "I suppose you will be restored to your rank in the military now?"

"No." He seemed to be struggling with words, as if he had forgotten how to speak English and assumed I no longer spoke Spanish. "I will not."

"Oh." I looked to the ground, where the magazine pages fluttered in a late afternoon breeze. I bent to collect the magazine and looked across the patio at his feet. The heavy, military boots were gone. He was wearing modern jogging shoes. "How did you find me?" I put the magazine on the chaise and indicated a chair beneath the patio umbrella.

He frowned. "Your Embassy acted on my behalf. A short time after the accord, I was brought to the consulate for interrogation. While I was in *Cuidad de Mexico,* I asked about you. I hope that was..." he glanced around again, "okay with you?"

"Oh..." it was my turn to look around. I felt like a six year old with a crush on the little boy next door. Any minute now, one of us was going to punch the other one on the shoulder and run. "Of-of course."

His eyes swept back to mine, and held me prisoner in his gaze. "Tell me, did you follow my instructions?"

"Instructions?" I repeated blankly. He was here. He was actually standing before me. He was a ghost, but he was here.

"I told you-"

Oh, yes, he had instructed me to remarry. "Oh, no, Javier. I couldn't. You see, I..." How could I explain? "It's a good thing I didn't, don't you think?"

He responded with a narrow eyed scowl. "I have never asked you to do anything that your life did not depend upon."

"I didn't know that marriage would save my life," I retorted, irritably. "A woman doesn't need a man to…oh, Javier, why did you come?" This wasn't the way it was supposed to be.

I didn't expect to see amusement, possibly even relief, in his expression as he reached into his back pocket. "I came to give you this." He held out the green billed cap that had been his symbol of betrothal.

I grabbed for it, impulsively. "Oh! You got it back for me." I pressed it to my breast. "I wanted to turn back for it when it fell off, but," I twisted away to brush the tears from my face, "you told me not to look back."

"I saw that, Dinah."

I jerked around. "You watched me go?"

Something inside him seemed to crumble, his military bearing, his arrogance, his resolve to keep his distance. "I have been watching you run away from me for months. I try to sleep and I see your hair flying as my…as this…" he gestured faintly toward the cap in my hands. "I said the war is over, Dinah, and you won." He dropped to his knees in front of me, reaching for my hand and pressing it to his lips. "The memories you left behind lured me over the border like a fish to a hook. I sought asylum from your Embassy."

"I…I can't believe it. I never thought you'd ever ask a favor from any government."

"I never thought I would. Until I met you, I never thought I would ask a favor of anyone." He rocked back on his heels and stared, unseeing, into the arbor. "The officials at the Embassy tried to tell me where you were. It seems, somehow, our good Padre had notified someone that we were married in the eyes of the

Church, and they felt I ought to know where my wife ended up. I did not let them tell me – at first. I wanted you to go and live again. But, in the end, I could not bear it and I went to the Bishop in Cuidad de Mexico, and found the proof of our marriage. With that, your Embassy arranged a visa and transportation."

He lifted his eyes to mine, and I gasped at the sight of his tears. "I surrender, *mi esposa*, my little rebel wife," he sighed. "There were so many times I thought I could teach you discipline and regimentation, yet all that time you were secretly teaching me the love of freedom that you embraced as passionately as I embraced you. So, now...here I am. I have no money. I have no home or future. I have nothing to give you but a great love. Will you have your revenge, now, rebel? Will you turn me away as thoughtlessly as I turned away poor beggars in the street?"

I drew a deep, shaky breath; it might have been my first since he appeared before me. My heart was soaring somewhere over my head. "No, *mi corazon,*" I took his hands and turned them upward. "I will fill those empty hands. Close your eyes."

"Dinah." He gaped at me. "Do not torture me."

"Close them," I commanded, adopting a tone I'd heard him use so many times.

"Very well." He sighed, as if my demands were a childish game, but his hands trembled as he held them, outstretched, all the same.

I moved to the other side of the chaise and gathered Jay up carefully and quietly, to lay him in his father's arms.

"Dinah," he whispered, not opening his eyes. "What is this game you are playing?"

"It's not a game, I assure you. Captain Contreras, please meet Javier David Contreras y McKee." I kissed his brow, softly. "I call him Jay."

"Jay?" he repeated. "Not-no, it does not matter." He opened his eyes and assessed the bundle in his arms. "He is so new," he whispered, awestruck. He drew the infant into the cradle of one arm, and gingerly touched one tiny fist with his fingertip.

"Eight days old," I told him.

"And he is..." he was struggling with emotion I had only glimpsed at Roberto's death, "my son?"

"*Si, tu jito.*"

"*Dios mio,*" he breathed. "You left knowing you would bear my child." Tears spilled down his cheeks. "How could you do that?"

I wiped at the tears, clumsily. "I tried to tell you, but you wouldn't let me. Believe me, Javier, I tried." I felt my own tears burning my eyes. "You sent me away."

"If I had known, Dinah." He looked over my head, to the arbor I had described to him. I could see him comparing the reality to my description. "I can only thank God you were not alone."

I looked over his shoulder toward the kitchen window, where I could see my mother back away from the curtain. "In a way, I was alone. My parents didn't want me to keep him. They didn't understand."

"Understand?" He was barely listening to me.

"They didn't understand how much I loved you." I held my breath, waiting for his mockery, his derision, even his doubt. I only saw a muscle twitch at his neck. He kept looking at the baby. "I kept my promise all those months, Javier. I finally told my mother today, because I couldn't bear for her to hate Jay."

He still did not look up, but a small smile creased his cheek. "That is what you would call good timing. I stood outside this magnificent house for a long time, not knowing if I would be allowed to enter." He looked up again, his eyes going everywhere. "Such a magnificent house," he repeated. "I have nothing like this to give you."

"It's just a house," I said, shrugging. Oh, I knew it was magnificent. I had my eyes opened for me down in those jungles. I had seen the truth, been forced to recognize my privilege. But it had always been just a house to me.

"Compared to a tent? To a cave?" He nodded toward the house. "This is a palace. A palace I did not feel worthy to enter. But," awkwardly, trying not to disturb his sleeping son, he reached into his pocket again, and pulled out a very worn photograph, "I kept looking at this until I had the strength to ring the bell." He held it out.

It was the photograph I had given him in those last precious hours. It was tattered and bent at the corners, and it looked as if the image had nearly been rubbed off the paper. I wanted to weep all over again.

He reached for it, looking as if it pained him to have it out of his possession. "I think I would have preferred a firing squad to those few moments waiting, and then that woman – your mother – came to the door. I could see the whole of your life play out on her face.

She didn't want to let me in, but it was clear she knew she had no choice. You look much like her. Beautiful." He tucked the photo back into his pocket. "If I never told you before. You are."

"Please." I tried to take Jay from his arms. "Stand up. Or…sit down. Don't stay there on the ground."

He let me take the baby, but he didn't like it. He stood, and when I pointed to a chair, he went to sit, and bounced up again, quickly. "You just came from *cama de parto*." He pointed to the chair. "You should not be standing so long. Should you be outside?"

"Oh, now *you* look like my mother," I sighed, and took another chair. "I daresay she was actually glad to see you." I shifted Jay in my arms. "She believes children should be near their fathers."

"And so do I," Javier agreed.

"I never thought you'd come," I said again. "I thought you were dead. And even if you weren't, I never dreamed you would come here for me." I felt the tears yet again and I turned away, blinking. "You told me you would find s-someone else to love."

Javier bounced out of his chair and turn my face to him. "How could I ever love anyone else, Dinah? I had no heart left with which to love? I love you, Dinah. Perhaps I should have said that long ago, too. "

"Perhaps…" my voice sounded weak and I coughed slightly. "Perhaps you didn't know?"

"I knew." He nodded. "I cannot say when I knew it, I only know how I felt the day I pulled you out of that crowd of my own soldiers. I admired you." He gestured. "And yes, I desired you. I thought you would be an easy conquest, but you fought me. Not just about…" there was unexpected color in his face. I might have laughed if I weren't drowning in emotion. "You fought me in all things. I tried to punish you, break you, and nearly broke myself in trying. The night I found you had gone back to help that woman deliver her child-" his eyes dropped to Jay "-I went insane with fear. I knew where you were. I knew how to find you and when I found you I was going to teach you never to defy me again. When I got to that hut and saw...what I saw...*Dios*, Dinah, your grief and anger was hanging in that hovel like smoke. It consumed me. It made me drunk with rage for you, at you, at the world. Then to come on those men with their hands on you-"

"Javier, please," I implored. "I've spent six months trying to forget that."

His voice softened but the hard expression remained. "Forgive me. Death was an everyday event to me. Forgive me," he repeated. "I have only recently been able to understand the terror of those weeks and months you spent with me. You were so brave. Someone at the Embassy called you a hero, but I did not need to be told. Savagery makes men savage...but not you. You fought to tame it, change it, but you would never give in to it."

"Javier," I began, but I didn't know where to go from there. His contrition caused me pain but I couldn't stop him. Because he felt it, he had become more human, more of the man I loved.

"You bore everything with patience and strength," he continued, as if compelled to finish the speech he'd begun. "The danger, the hardship, my anger when I lashed out at you, unable to understand what you were doing to me. And when you were gone, I realized it – you made me need you." Suddenly he was pulling me from the chair, embracing me. "Dinah," he whispered against my mouth. "I have needed you so long."

I was trembling, too…or perhaps it was Jay squirming between us. But, it wasn't Jay who made my knees weak or reminded me of that desire I thought I'd buried when I was trying to bury the memories of Javier. "Let me put him in his basket before one of us drops him," I said, pulling away, shakily.

Javier followed me to the woven bassinet my mother had placed in the shade on the other side of the chaise where I had been resting. He watched me tuck the baby in amongst fluffy white wool of my old layette blanket. "He is a handsome boy," he observed.

I straightened and admired the baby. "He looks like you."

Putting his hands on my shoulders, he turned me and kissed me and there was so much in that kiss – for both of us. Hunger, desire, passion, loneliness, neediness, fear and seven months of long, lonely nights. "Dinah, I want you so much. There has been no one since you left…not in my hands, not in my heart, not even in here." He touched his temple. "The idea of touching another woman...no, I could not even think it." His hands fell to his sides, abruptly. "I forget we are not alone in the middle of a jungle, where we can make love whenever we wish." He swung slightly to the left, and his dark eyes swept up to the windows of the house the same way they once scanned roads and hillsides for danger.

I pointed, boldly. "That's my bedroom," I told him, with a smile that was anything but coy.

"Your parents..."

"Wouldn't dream of interfering," I promised. "I'm pretty sure my mom would even look after Jay for a while, if we wanted to be alone."

He looked back to the bassinet. "He's so new," he said thoughtfully. "Is it safe to-"

"Don't you dare, Javier," I warned. "Don't you dare kiss me like that, say things like that and then try to make excuses. If the idea of making love in my father's house makes you uncomfortable, we'll go to a hotel. But," I waited until his eyes met mine, "I'm afraid it's unlikely we'll ever get another room with a waterfall."

He shook his head as he pulled me back into his arms. "I do not need a waterfall, *mi jita*. All I require is you."

"And you have me," I promised, throwing my arms around him, kissing him deeply, as he had taught me, again and again.

And again he pulled back, unwinding my arms from his neck. "What is it?" I demanded.

"I cannot stay," he said, miserably. "My visa is for a very short time. I did not expect to find..." his eyes flicked to the basket and back. "I just wanted to know that you were recovering and...and happy. I was not expecting this kind of reception. I did not even plan to talk to you and I wasted so many days convincing myself not to see you, even though that's all I wanted to do. Now, I must go."

"Go?" I repeated, devastated. "Don't you want to stay?" I pushed back, as if I expected him to touch me again. "Why did you even come, Javier? Why did come here and say those things-"

He cut me off with a brutal kiss. "I lied," he said fiercely. "I did not want to find you happy in the arms of another man, but I did not come prepared for any other way. Now, I must go back to Cuidad de Mexico and apply for another visa. Even married to a United States citizen, it will take some time." His arms tightened around me. "I do not know how I will bear it."

"We'll work it out," I promised, smoothing his hair back from his eyes. "Maybe Daddy knows someone, or Jay and I can come with you, and wait for the visa to be approved. I don't care. We don't even have to come back...if, that's what you want."

Javier shook his head. "You have so much here and I have nothing. I cannot ask you to give it up for me."

"You cannot ask me to give up you," I corrected, firmly. "There's a way, Javier. We've survived this much, we'll find a way. "

Javier tugged at his lower lip, thoughtfully. "I discovered that I have some family in Mexico. They might welcome someone to help manage their ranches."

"That would be fine," I promised him. "Didn't I just say that I'll go anywhere you want me to be? I'll go back to living in caves, if that's where you want to be."

"No caves, Dinah. Not for our son. Son," he repeated. "This family...they have some money, but they have no sons." He pulled himself away from his thoughts. "But, you are a nurse. Where would you practice your vocation?"

"What about you? You're a soldier. Would you be content herding cows? I can do it if you can. And what a chance for our son, to grow up as part of a dynasty." The doubt was still evident in his eyes, in his frown. "I told you, Javier, we've already survived war and poverty and death and separation and-"

He put a hand up, reminding me of the soldier he had been. "That is the past, Dinah. The past is over. We will never speak of it again. For now, from this moment, we think only of the future. We will think only of our love, our marriage, our son. Our son," he said again, his voice edged in wonder. "Gloria de Dios, our son will not grow up with poverty and death as his inheritance, no matter where we live, because his mother, my rebel wife, will teach him what it means to be free. Just as she freed me." He kissed me under the arbor and the sunshine and, at last, we were both free.

The End

About the Author

Perle Butcher Lyon is a former historian and educator whose stories revisit watershed periods of history from a very personal perspective.

Other books by Perle Butcher Lyon:

The Wreck of the Sidonie Stone
The Dutch Doctor

More From Inknbeans Press

If you enjoyed this book, please visit Inknbeans.com and discover our other fine authors.

www.ingramcontent.com/pod-product-compliance
Lightning Source LLC
Chambersburg PA
CBHW060414180626
46817CB00007B/2573

* 9 7 8 0 6 9 2 5 8 1 1 3 1 *